"Exactly what game are you playing, Gemma?"

The very softness of Logan's voice was frightening. Gemma sat down on the bed, her knees too weak to support her.

"It isn't a game. I haven't thought of an audition in days —I don't want one now if it means losing you—"

"You just lost the lot," he said brutally. "I don't like being used, Gemma. You knew who I was and you gave me the performance of your career that night—what an opportunity for an actress! I doubt you'll ever be better."

"Logan," she whispered. "I wanted you to make love to me —I didn't do it just for the part—"

"You're a liar," he said, and looking into his eyes she knew everything was over between them.

Books by Kay Thorpe

HARLEQUIN PRESENTS

242—CARIBBEAN ENCOUNTER
299—BITTER ALLIANCE
311—THE MAN FROM TRIPOLI
336—THIS SIDE OF PARADISE
360—THE DIVIDING LINE
378—CHANCE MEETING
394—NO PASSING FANCY
425—FLOODTIDE
455—COPPER LAKE
491—TEMPORARY WIFE
534—THE NEW OWNER
573—A MAN OF MEANS
597—MASTER OF MORLEY
646—THE LAND OF THE INCAS
678—NEVER TRUST A STRANGER

HARLEQUIN ROMANCES

1583—SAWDUST SEASON
1609—NOT WANTED ON VOYAGE
1661—OLIVE ISLAND
1756—AN APPLE IN EDEN
1779—THE MAN AT KAMBALA
1909—THE SHIFTING SANDS
1967—SUGAR CANE HARVEST
1990—THE ROYAL AFFAIR
2046—SAFARI SOUTH
2079—THE RIVER LORD
2109—STORM PASSAGE
2151—TIMBER BOSS
2232—THE WILDERNESS TRAIL
2234—FULL CIRCLE

These books may be available at your local bookseller.

For a free catalog listing all titles currently available,
send your name and address to:

Harlequin Reader Service
P.O. Box 52040, Phoenix, AZ 85072-2040
Canadian address: Stratford, Ontario N5A 6W2

KAY THORPE

never trust a stranger

Harlequin Books

TORONTO • NEW YORK • LONDON
AMSTERDAM • PARIS • SYDNEY • HAMBURG
STOCKHOLM • ATHENS • TOKYO • MILAN

Harlequin Presents first edition March 1984
ISBN 0-373-10678-5

Original hardcover edition published in 1983
by Mills & Boon Limited

CHAPTER ONE

'SORRY I can't take you any further,' said the lorry driver regretfully, pulling in to the kerb. 'The southbound ramp is right over there. You shouldn't be long getting another lift. Just watch who you get in with, that's all. Can't be too careful these days, love!'

Gemma smiled at the man, aware that his concern was not without foundation. 'Don't worry,' she said, 'I will. Thanks for coming this far out of your way.'

'No trouble,' he denied as she lowered herself to the ground. 'Enjoyed the company. Hope you soon find yourself another show!'

He wasn't alone in that, acknowledged Gemma, raising a hand in farewell as the vehicle moved off. It wasn't going to be easy at this time of year, that was for sure. A summer season in a small, draughty theatre on the east coast might not be very far up the ladder in theatrical terms, but she had at least believed herself secure until September was out. The weather hadn't helped. It had been the worst July in years. Playing to near-empty houses night after night was hardly scheduled to lift anybody's bank balance, the manager had ruefully pointed out on announcing the premature closure.

Where money was concerned, Gemma knew she could always fall back on the account credited each month by transfer from New York, but that would only be in case of dire need, she told herself now with resolution. Her mother had supported her through stage school: that was more than enough. She had to stand on her own feet, even if it meant taking a job outside the theatre until something turned up. Always providing she could get one of those, of course. Dancing and drama diplomas were of little importance to the average employer.

It started to drizzle with rain as she turned on to the motorway access ramp. Tucking her long dark hair into her anorak hood, she made a hopeful gesture at an oncoming car, relaxing again wryly as it went right on past without decreasing speed. People could hardly be blamed for reluctance to pick up free-wheeling passengers after hearing so many horror stories of resulting muggings. On the other hand, at five feet five and little more than eight stone, she was surely not the stuff of which muggers were made?

Looking down at herself, she had to admit that her appearance was little help. The anorak was old, her jeans frankly tatty and her duffle bag had seen better days too. Clothes had become of secondary interest in her life. Three years at the Academy, followed by a couple of months in a seaside pier show, hardly called for an extensive wardrobe. There had hardly been room in the bed-sitter which had been home for so long anyway.

Thinking back, it seemed a lot more than five years since her parents' divorce. Even now she found it difficult to accept that her father had a new wife and growing family. She got along quite well with Shirley, and she knew she was always welcome at their home in Southampton, but her visits were few and far between. Jealousy was the problem—an emotion she couldn't help. He's *my* father, she always wanted to shout at the twin boys as they clambered over him on his return from work in the evenings, which was more than a little ridiculous, considering their age.

They were a very close-knit family; closer than Gemma could remember her own family unit had ever been. She blamed her mother for that, yet she supposed one should consider the mitigating factors. Marriage at seventeen and motherhood less than a year later allowed little opportunity for growing up with a balanced outlook. The stage had called with a louder voice than any family commitments.

Professionally, her fame now at forty was well merited. A star of international repute, she was at present in the final week of a long Broadway run acclaimed by all. Gemma had not seen her for almost a year, and did not expect to do so in the immediate future. There would be another show lined up; there always was. Only if there was a tempting enough offer from this side of the Atlantic would she be likely to return.

Had any of her fellow pupils at the Academy known of her connection with Adele Berrisford they would have thought her a fool for not capitalising on the fact, but the last thing she wanted was recognition of that nature. Having spent the better part of her life basking in reflected glory, she made a point of keeping the relationship secret wherever possible—a task made easier by her mother's reversion to her maiden name for professional purposes.

Comparisons were inevitable. They always had been. Adele Berrisford was not only a fine performer, she was also a very beautiful woman. Gemma had been called attractive herself, but she could never compete. She didn't want to compete. Her love of the stage might have been inherited from her mother, but if she made it at all it had to be through her own individual talent, or where was the satisfaction?

The silver-grey Mercedes coming up the ramp was slowing, left indicator flashing to signal a pull-in to the kerb edge. Gemma hoisted her duffle bag further up her shoulder and stepped forward, scarcely believing her luck. Cars like this one rarely stopped to pick up hitch-hikers, particularly where the would-be passenger was damp and bedraggled from the rain. If the driver proved to be going all the way through to London too she would really start to trust in the zodiac readings. 'An unexpected event will prove advantageous', her horoscope had said that morning. Perhaps it was a good omen for the future too.

Opening the passenger door, she slid into the seat, stowing the duffle bag at her feet before turning to look at the driver with a word of thanks as he put the car into motion again.

'Where are you making for?' he asked.

'London,' she said, fastening the seat-belt.

'Then you're in luck. I'm going all the way through.'

'Oh, great! It isn't exactly the weather for standing around.'

He made no answer to that, watching his door mirror as they came down on to the run-in lane.

Turned a little in her seat, Gemma studied him with interest. Early to mid-thirties, she guessed, and obviously not short of money. The car apart, his shadow-striped dark suit sat his broad-shouldered frame the way only fine tailoring could. Standing, he would be over the six feet mark for certain, and fit with it. The dark, crisply styled hair suited his strongly defined features. A man of decision, she judged: a man whose masculinity would never be in doubt. That lower lip of his betrayed a certain sensuality of line, arousing a quiver of awareness deep down in the pit of her stomach.

At this hour of the morning the motorway traffic was heavy. Seizing his chance, her benefactor put his foot down and slid into a gap between two lorries, moving over almost immediately into the middle lane and from there into the outer in order to overtake a slower moving car. Gemma stayed silent until he had completed the manoeuvre and was once more back in the centre lane, settling into her seat with the confidence born of knowing she was in good hands.

'We seem to have hit the busy time,' she remarked rather obviously. 'I'd as soon take a longer route as try to compete with this kind of traffic myself!'

'If it scares you, you'd be right to do that,' he agreed on a faint note of derision. 'Driving isn't a pastime for the nervous—not in this day and age.'

She had asked for that, Gemma conceded ruefully. She had been talking just for the sake of something to say. Kind-hearted enough to offer her a lift he might be, but he was obviously not in the habit of suffering fools gladly. It was too late to start denying the implication now. What she would do was watch her tongue from here-on-in.

'Do you do this kind of thing often?' he asked after a moment or two, not taking his eyes from the road ahead.

'Do what—oh, you mean hitch-hike?' She shook her head, realised he was unlikely to have seen the gesture and hastily added, 'Only when necessary. British Rail will soon have priced themselves out of existence.'

'There are coaches to London from most cities. They're cheaper, I believe.'

'A lot,' she agreed. 'Only I can find a better use for the money.'

There was a pause before he spoke again. 'You're going to London to look for a job?'

'Yes.' It was a true enough answer, if a little incomplete. Her business was her own.

'The streets aren't paved with gold, you know.' The derisive note was back. 'Good jobs are as scarce there as anywhere else. I'm assuming you've somewhere to stay till you find something?'

'I thought of the Y.W.C.A.,' she murmured, resenting his attitude even while she saw the sense in what he was saying. 'It's cheap and it's handy.'

'And safe. That's a big consideration for a girl on her own.'

Gemma laughed. 'Oh, I can take care of myself! I've been doing it for years.'

'Really?' The inflection was dry. 'And I suppose if I turned out to be a rapist you'd deal with that too?'

'If necessary.' He was deliberately mocking her, but she was not about to let him put her down. 'Not that it ever would be. I'm a good enough judge of character to make darn sure I didn't get into a car with anyone who appeared in the least doubtful.'

'You believe the soul is reflected in the eyes?'

'I believe evil is.' Her shrug held deliberation. 'Anyway, I know enough about male physiology to give any would-be rapist a nasty shock. A knee is a useful weapon!'

'Providing you got the chance to use it. You might find it difficult flat on your back.'

'I'd hardly let things get that far, would I?' She made no effort to keep the sarcasm from her voice. 'Look, Mr——?'

'Telford,' he supplied. 'Logan Telford.'

'Mr Telford. I realise you're probably only trying to be helpful, but I really can look after myself! Please don't worry about me.'

'Fine.' He sounded not in the least put out. 'If that's the way you'd prefer it.'

'Yes, it is.' Gemma tried to lighten the words, aware that she owed this man politeness if only in gratitude for the lift. 'I'm used to independence. I've had it for more than three years.'

'No parents?'

'Divorced.' Her tone was short. 'I don't think you really want to hear my life history, do you.' It was a statement, not a question. 'How long will it take into London?'

'Depending on the traffic we hit, anything between two and three hours.' If he resented her attitude he wasn't showing it. 'You don't have to be there for a certain time, do you?'

'No, my time's my own. Did you intend stopping for lunch?'

'Hadn't got round to thinking about it yet,' he admitted. 'Hungry?'

'A bit.' She added swiftly, 'I do have enough money to pay for my own meal.'

His mouth took on a slant. 'That's comforting. It's half eleven now. Supposing we stop at the next Services? I'm going to need some petrol anyway.'

'Fine by me.' Gemma was already feeling more than a little ashamed of her bad manners. Retraction, however, would only bring the subject of her background under scrutiny again, and that she didn't want. Best to just leave it alone. He didn't seem to care anyway.

There was silence after that, broken only by the well-insulated hum of the engine and muted traffic noise. Gemma would have liked to ask to have the radio on, but didn't quite have the nerve considering her approach to his conversational overtures. It was going to be a long journey unless they found something to talk about. Some impersonal subject shouldn't be all that difficult to come up with.

She was still thinking about it when he pulled over into the slow lane, leaving the indicator flashing to signal that he was leaving the motorway at the coming exit.

'I just remembered a rather good little pub half a mile down the road here,' he said by way of explanation. 'The food is better than any we'll get in the Services' snack bars, and a proper restaurant meal is going to take too long. There's a petrol station too, so we can kill two birds with one stone.' Just for a moment the line of his mouth suggested a certain unwonted cynicism. 'Half an hour, and we'll be on our way again.'

Gemma relaxed. A pub lunch sounded just the thing—and it would be cheap. No matter what, she was going to pay for her own meal. She was under enough of an obligation to this Logan Telford as it was. Oddly, the name seemed somehow familiar, yet she had definitely never met him before. Had she not been quite so ready to cut out communication between them herself she could have asked him what he did for a living. Not that it really mattered so much. Once this journey was over they were unlikely ever to meet again.

It was a long half mile, she found herself thinking a few minutes later as they turned from the main road on to a narrow lane with nothing in sight but trees and grassland. This pub, whatever it was called, was right off the beaten track. The rain had stopped some miles back, but the sky hung grey and heavy overhead, lending the whole scene a melancholy look. A typical English August, Gemma thought dryly. If it wasn't for the fact that fine days in this country of theirs were finer than anywhere else in the world, who would stay?

The sudden turn-in through an open gateway on to a rutted track took her by surprise. She was even more surprised when her companion stopped the car and turned off the engine instead of backing out of what was obviously a wrong turning.

'Don't tell me they knocked your pub down,' she said with a little laugh. 'That would be a shame!'

'There isn't any pub—at least not in the immediate area.' His tone was perfectly level. 'If you still feel like eating afterwards, I'll take you to it with pleasure.'

'Afterwards?' She looked at him with a faint frown, seeing him full face for the first time. Grey eyes, she noted irrelevantly: cold like steel at present—and a little frightening. Something tautened ominously in her chest. 'I'm not sure what you're trying to say,' she began, 'but I——'

'Remember what we were talking about earlier?' he asked. 'Didn't it ever occur to you that I might have brought the subject up with purpose?' He shook his head mockingly at the look in her own widened green eyes, unfastening his seat-belt at the same time. 'So much confidence deserves to be put to the test!'

Gemma attempted to twist her body away from him as he reached towards her, but the belt restricted her movements. The hands on her upper arms were iron-hard; irresistible in their strength. She caught the subtle aroma of aftershave as he brought his mouth down on hers, then her mind emptied of everything but the degradation of having her lips forced apart, her breast encircled by fingers totally lacking in gentleness or finesse. One of her hands was trapped between her body and the seat; when she attempted to use the other to scratch at his face he simply caught her wrist and pinioned it behind her back before returning to his assault, this time sliding his hand inside her anorak and the shirt she wore beneath to find bare flesh.

'Useful!' he murmured against her mouth. 'That makes less to take off. Stop struggling—it isn't going to get you anywhere. I think we can say we've proved that much pretty fully.'

'Let me go!' The command was supposed to sound strong and authoritative, but the quiver in her voice gave her away. 'What do you think you're doing?'

'The thing you said no one would ever get close enough to you to do,' he returned with irony, leaving his hand right where it was. 'If I press this button here on the console the seat backs will go down flat. Do you still think you can handle the situation?'

So that was what it was all about—a lesson in over-confidence. Relief was her first reaction, followed in short order by a seething anger.

'Get your hands off me!' she snapped. 'And keep them off!'

His mouth twisted. 'Still not convinced, are you? All right, you asked for it! I can't say I'll find the experience any trial. You're hiding a whole lot of feminine charm under all this beatnik gear! Getting you out of it is going to be like opening an unexpected Christmas present.'

There was no stopping the steely fingers loosing the buckle of her belt. Anger gave way to a whole turmoil of emotions as he pulled her shirt free and slid warm hands over the bare skin of her back. He was serious. He really was serious! Worse than that was the response she could feel rising in her. He was a total stranger, for heaven's sake!

'No.' This time she used a different tone, voice low, and lacking in bravado. 'All right, you've convinced me. Let me go—please!'

He did so immediately, sitting back in his seat

to watch her straighten her clothing with sardonic satisfaction. 'You needed that,' he said, 'if only to show you what a young idiot you are! How many times do girls your age have to get themselves raped or worse before you start to learn common sense?'

'You picked me up,' she muttered defensively.

'Meaning people like me encourage you to do it? Fair comment, except that I picked you up with the sole purpose of keeping you out of possible trouble.'

Green eyes flashed. 'Am I supposed to thank you for what you just did?'

'No,' he said, 'just remember it. You could easily be lying there strangled right this moment, and little you could have done to stop it. Never take anyone at face value. It's too dangerous.'

'You made your point.' This was one time when her acting experience stood her in good stead. Not for anything was she going to let him see just how badly he had shaken her. She made herself shrug and smile. 'I suppose I did drop myself in for it. Does that offer to take me to lunch still stand?'

He studied her for a lengthy moment, an odd expression in his eyes. 'I'll say one thing for you,' he stated at last, 'you're not easily put down. I'm not sure whether that's a good thing or bad.' Straightening, he switched on the ignition and reached for his seat-belt. 'Lunch it is.'

Gemma stayed silent as he reversed the car out of the gate and back on to the lane, emotions in a spin. Her skin tingled where the long lean fingers had touched her, and she could still feel the imprint of his lips. For the first time in years she actually regretted her casual approach to the way she looked. A beatnik, he had called her. An outdated term maybe, but it conjured up an image that was anything but flattering. Certainly the women in which he took a normal interest would not dress in faded jeans and scruffy anoraks. They would be beautiful, sophisticated creatures with salon-styled hair and immaculate make-up; the kind of women other men would envy him.

What was wrong with her anyway? she asked herself reprehensively at that point. This man had just attacked her! Whatever his motives there had been no excuse for going as far as he had.

The public house he had spoken of turned out to be over three miles in the opposite direction to the one they had taken. It was only a small place, but it served an excellent choice of meals on a plate. Logan ordered a beer for himself while they waited to eat, accepting Gemma's refusal of a drink without argument.

Standing by his side at the bar while they studied the menu, she was acutely conscious of the interest they were arousing among the other clientele. On the face of it they made an oddly assorted pair, she had to acknowledge. At a couple of inches over six feet, Logan Telford would have stood out in any crowd. In the low-beamed bar he seemed to tower.

The hand holding the menu was long and fleshless, nails short-cut but obviously tended with expert care. A wafer-thin gold watch showed beneath one crisp white cuff, nestling amidst the light covering of dark hairs on his wrist. It was the same hand he had used on her not half an hour previously. Gemma forcibly controlled the tremor that very memory sent coursing through her. It wouldn't be happening again, that was for sure. He had taught her the lesson he had set out to teach her. From now on she was simply a liability he could no doubt barely wait to despatch.

They sat down to eat at one of the corner tables when their meal finally arrived. Gemma had taken off her anorak on entering, owing to the warmth of the room. Only now did she notice the tear in the sleeve of her check gingham shirt. Too late to try hiding it. Logan Telford would have noticed; he was the kind to notice everything. Why worry anyway? She was what she was. Wishing wouldn't change anything.

He made no attempt to converse during the following moments, seemingly preoccupied with his thoughts. Only when coffee was brought to the table did he appear to recall her presence, sitting back in his seat to view her with faintly lifted brows.

'Better?'

'If you mean am I hungry any more, the answer is no,' she said.

A smile touched his lips. 'I'm not going to do any apologising.'

Gemma eyed him back unflinchingly. 'I shouldn't imagine you do too much of that at any time. Why make an exception for me?'

'Cute,' he said. 'As full of bounce as a rubber ball!'

'What did you expect—total abjection?' She shook her head. 'Sorry, it isn't my style.'

'It was being so damned clever that got you

into trouble in the first place,' he reminded her softly. 'Don't you benefit from experience?'

'Only where it has any value. I didn't——' She caught the look in his eyes and paused suddenly, biting her lip. 'You didn't have to go as far as you did.'

'No,' he agreed surprisingly, 'I didn't. Perhaps I got a little too deeply into the role.'

It was his choice of phrase that stimulated her memory. Logan Telford. Of course! She should have known at once. He had produced *Cool Generation* last year. Everyone from the Academy who had seen the show, including herself, had thought it excellent, but the public had stayed away in droves. It had been taken off after a bare seven-week run, which meant a lot of money must have been lost. So far as she was aware, it had been his first failure on the London stage. She doubted if he would appreciate being reminded of it now.

Reputedly, he was in the process of financing a new stage version of *Kiss Me, Kate* at present. Excitement stirred in her at the thought. Could this possibly be the advantage her horoscope had promised her? True, the producer normally played but a nominal part in the casting of minor roles, but that wasn't to say he couldn't recommend. To even get as far as an audition would be something. At least she had her Equity card now. For that alone the last couple of months had been worthwhile.

The elation lasted bare moments. Her performance to date was hardly scheduled to impress him, was it? No matter how she might feel about his behaviour she had to retrieve the situation somehow. She summoned a smile.

'To be honest, I feel an absolute idiot. Could we agree to forget it?'

His answering smile was slow and somewhat dry. 'Start again, you mean?'

Her heart jerked suddenly. 'Please,' she said.

'That's fine by me.' His eyes moved over her face with thoughtful, almost calculating expression; she could sense him come to some kind of decision. 'I've a proposition for you,' he added unexpectedly. 'No——' seeing her own expression undergo a swift alteration—'not that kind. This is a job. I need someone to act as my fiancée for the coming weekend.'

Gemma stared at him, scarcely able to believe she had heard him right. 'Are you serious?'

'Never more.' He took a gold cigarette case from an inside pocket and offered it opened across the table, taking one for himself when she refused and thumbing the inbuilt lighter into flame. The smoke wreathed between them as he continued. 'Obviously I don't expect to hire your services for nothing. We can come to a mutually satisfying arrangement.'

'I don't understand.' Gemma still couldn't take it in. 'Why on earth should you need to hire a bogus fiancée?'

'Expediency,' he said. 'To cut a long story short, I'm presently raising backing for a show I'm to produce. In theatre talk, backers are called angels. This weekend I'm planning on nailing Gabriel himself, with any luck!' He shook his head as she attempted to say something. 'No, let me finish. The man has a new wife. She's twenty-five years younger than he is.' The grey eyes were steady. 'He knows she and I were acquainted before he met her, and he's a very jealous and possessive man. If I go out to the house this weekend without a woman of my own in tow he might let that jealousy get the better of his business sense. Understand?'

'Yes,' Gemma conceded slowly. 'But surely you must know plenty of women who'd be only too glad to help you out, without having to ask a complete stranger?'

His lips twisted. 'Not without expecting rather more than I'm prepared to give in return. Ours would be purely a business arrangement.' Once again his gaze moved over her, taking on a certain resignation. 'Obviously there would have to be some changes made. You're going to need the right clothes, for one thing—and something done with your hair: it's a mess.'

'Thanks.' Her tone was cool. 'Aren't you taking a little too much for granted? I haven't said I'll do it.'

'But you're going to.' There was cynicism in his regard. 'It's too good a chance to miss. I'll pay you enough to keep you going for a few weeks until you find yourself a job. I'm not going to pretend you're the ideal material. Beggars can't be choosers, that's all. In the right hands you can be made to look the part, and I think you have enough confidence in yourself to act the part. It's only going to be for a couple of days. After that we each go our own way.'

He was right, Gemma had to concede, smothering resentment before it was fully born, it was too good a chance to miss—only not for the reasons he had stated. The excitement was stirring again, every nerve in her body stretched to the familiar pre-performance tension. If she could put on a good enough act in this role offered her she would be more than halfway towards a possible audition for the show itself. Perhaps she could even make it a condition of acceptance. Rejection of that latter idea came swiftly. Logan Telford was not the kind of man one could coerce in that fashion. It would be far better to make the impression before even telling him she was in the business herself. That way she would have a basis to build on.

'If you really think I can do it, I'll take you up on it,' she said, and laughed. 'After all, I don't have anything very much else to do!'

From the fleeting expression in his eyes, he was already half regretting the offer. He stubbed out the barely begun cigarette in the glass tray and pushed back his chair with a decisive gesture. 'In that case we'd better get started. It's going to be a busy afternoon.'

CHAPTER TWO

IT was almost three by the time they reached town. Logan made straight for the King's Road, parking the car on a side street to walk Gemma back a few hundred yards to an exclusive-looking boutique called Elizabeth's.

Inappropriately, the red-haired and extremely attractive proprietress was named Sally Rogers. She and Logan greeted each other in the manner of old friends. He performed a brief introduction and an equally brief explanation of his requirements, the latter eliciting a smile of comprehension and a speculative glance in Gemma's direction from the woman.

'One of these days you're going to get what's coming to you,' she remarked without malice. 'What time do you need her?'

'Not until tomorrow afternoon,' he said. Only then did he turn back to Gemma, expression coolly businesslike. 'I'll book you a room at the Inter-Continental for tonight, and pick you up at three in the lobby. Don't be late.'

Gemma resisted the impulse to drop a curtsey, contenting herself with an inclination of the head by way of acknowledgement. The act didn't start until tomorrow, she gathered. Until then she was on her own. That was okay by her. It would give her time to get the feel of the part. They had discussed her supposed background on the way down, lending credence to her faint but still

discernible Hampshire accent by placing her
'family' in Winchester. She had met Logan
through her job as secretary with a theatrical
agency called Boston Enterprises, which actually
existed, and they had been engaged for three
months. Nothing too difficult there; in fact, it
seemed almost too easy. The two hundred
pounds Logan had offered her was going to be
money for jam—especially considering that she
got to keep the new wardrobe he was providing
into the bargain. If she could manage to swing
the audition too that would be filling the cup to
overflowing, but who would be complaining? As
to what might come of an audition, that was
another story. It was unlucky to plan too far
ahead.

Sally proved to be not only quick on the uptake
but swift to action also, turning over the shop to
one of her assistants as soon as Logan had left,
and whisking Gemma to a salon down the road
for attention to her hair before anything else.

'Give her the works,' she said, having
wheedled the establishment into fitting her in
without an appointment. 'A completely new
look!' To Gemma herself, she added, 'I'll be back
to get you in an hour or so, then we can start on
the rest.'

Seated before a mirror, Gemma watched the
young male stylist as he lifted the heavy fall of
dark hair from her shoulders and tried out a few
different shapes about her face, waiting for what
she knew was coming. She was not disappointed.

'It should be cut,' he declared. 'A shingle
would be ideal.'

'No, thanks.' Her tone was pleasant but firm. 'I

realise short hair is all the rage at the moment, only I prefer mine long.'

'It ruins the shape of your face,' he said, quite unperturbed by the refusal. 'You're just another nice-looking girl right now. With the right hairstyle you could be devastating!'

Gemma gazed at him for a moment, then looked back at her reflection, trying to assess his degree of sincerity. To lie for the sake of it would hardly be good policy on his part, as the finished product was the establishment's advertisement. But devastating!

'I won't go as far as a shingle,' she said at length with some hesitation, 'but you could cut some off if you like. Not too much, though!'

'Of course.' He was galvanised into instant action, snapping his fingers for scissors and clips. 'Just enough.'

Ricky's idea of 'just enough' and her own were obviously two totally different things, Gemma thought dryly some fifty minutes later, viewing herself in the mirror again. All the same, she had to concede that his idea was the better of the two. He had cut her hair on a level with the bottom of her ears all the way round, shaping the thickness into a faint undercurve and giving her a matching fringe down to her eyebrows. More of a bob than a shingle, and very Twenties in essence, yet what it did for her face was beyond belief! She looked like another person; she even felt different. A modern Cleopatra, was the only way to describe her new image.

Sally Rogers expressed the same disbelief when she returned, taking Gemma's chin in her hand to turn her face this way and that with an air of bemusement.

'He isn't going to know you!' she declared, sounding distinctly intrigued. 'You know, you're really quite lovely! I'm looking forward to dressing you.'

Which probably meant she hadn't been before, guessed Gemma shrewdly. Not that she could blame the woman. She was pretty overwhelmed with the new look herself.

She lost track of time after that, trying on garment after garment in a fitting room back at Elizabeth's until Sally herself was satisfied with the final results. Lingerie from a shop a few doors away came next, followed by a choice of several pairs of shoes with matching purses after closing time with the assistance of yet another of Sally's fashion-world associates.

Dropped off at the hotel around six-fifteen wearing a suit in dusky pink with grey accessories, Gemma crossed the lobby to the reception desk feeling she was already well into the part she was to play. The smile with which she was greeted by the young male receptionist was a sure boost to her ego. She smiled back with genuine warmth as she signed in, accepting his offer to provide a bellboy to carry her new suitcase with a total disregard for the cost of the tip she would be expected to give the latter on arrival at her room. After this weekend money would no longer be short; at least not immediately, and with luck in the long term too.

Only when she was alone at length in the large and airy bedroom did she begin to experience a sense of anti-climax. Here she was, all dressed up and nowhere to go. Dinner would take up some time, true, but it still left her with the majority of the evening to get through.

On impulse, she picked up the telephone and got through to the hotel's theatre reservation service, asking if they could obtain her a single ticket for any one of the big musicals, and accepting the asking price without flickering an eyelid. The show started at eight, which left her with just over an hour and fifteen minutes to change, have something to eat and make her way to the theatre for curtain up. She would stop at the reservation desk on the way out and settle for the ticket in cash, she promised herself. There was no reason why Logan Telford should be expected to pay for that too. The bill for tonight was extra as it was. He had already settled that much.

Out of the several garments Sally Rogers had deemed necessary to a country weekend, Gemma chose a semi-fitted dress in fine lilac crêpe which subtly outlined her slender curves. With it she wore the same grey accessories. Fine feathers make fine birds, she thought amusedly, studying her reflection in the mirror when she was ready to go. Who would connect this shining-haired, expensively dressed young woman with the girl who only this morning had plied for a lift like some destitute? Judging from Sally's reaction, it was going to be interesting to see the effect her changed appearance had on Logan tomorrow. Beggars couldn't be choosers indeed! Already she was acquiring a whole new personality to go with her image, building up from the inside out. Confidence was the keynote. From now on she let no one put her down!

She ate in the hotel, arriving at the theatre by taxi some ten minutes before curtain-rise. Her seat was on the front row of the dress circle at the end of the middle section. Apart from the odd seat here and there it was a full house. Sitting back as the lights dimmed and the orchestra struck up the opening bars, Gemma gave herself over to the rare enjoyment of a spectator's role.

The interval found her keenly anticipatory of the second half—an enthusiasm shared by most, if the comments of those about her were anything to go by. She would have liked a drink of some kind, but the thought of facing a crowded bar was too off-putting. Instead she watched the audience below, supporting her weight on her elbows as she leaned forward.

As usual there was a lot of milling around, with some people blocking the gangways as they stopped to chat with friends and acquaintances. Gemma let her eyes wander idly along the rows, pausing here and there as some particular seat occupant caught her attention. She had always been fascinated by faces, especially when the mind behind them was unaware of being watched. That man down there in the left-hand section, for instance. From the look on his face he was thinking of things far removed from a relaxing night out at the theatre. Even as she watched she saw his lips move faintly, as if he were talking to himself.

Some people coming back down the aisle temporarily blocked her view. When she could see him again, the recipient of her interest had turned his head so that she could no longer view his face. Two rows in front of him the ashen hair of a woman in black caught the light as she moved. She was smiling as she looked at her companion, head tilted back as if in amusement at some remark made. Gemma shifted her gaze to the man in question and felt something jerk inside her. Coincidental that she and Logan Telford should have chosen to spend their evening at the same place. Not that his choice would have been made at the last minute, for certain. Aisle seats in the stalls were always well pre-booked.

He was laughing too, the chiselled features relaxed in a manner quite new to her. He was wearing a pale grey suit that outlined the breadth of his shoulders above the seat back. On first sight she had judged him a man who would have plenty of women around, so why should she feel this sense of depression about it right now? Their whole association was purely a business arrangement.

Regardless of the excellence of the production, she did not enjoy the second half nearly as much. Too well aware of the difficulty of getting a taxi when the theatres were turning out, and not fancying a tube or bus ride on her own late in the evening, she had taken the precaution of ordering a mini-cab to pick her up outside the theatre. Standing amid the milling throngs, trying to work out which of the many creeping or illegally parked vehicles might be her particular transport, she saw Logan and his companion emerge a short distance away along the pavement.

Even as she spotted them, Logan turned his head and looked directly at her, but no shadow of recognition crossed his features, although his glance lingered for a second or two before he moved off across the road with the blonde woman clinging possessively to an arm. Watching them go, Gemma felt the depression lift a little. Tomorrow was still to come. She wondered if he would remember this moment tonight when their eyes had so briefly met. It was going to be fun seeing the astonishment dawn.

She found her mini-cab eventually, arriving back at the hotel before eleven. It felt lonely in her room. She contemplated going back downstairs for a drink in one of the bars, but a girl on her own at this time of the evening was asking for trouble of one kind or another. Bed was the best solution. The sooner she slept, the sooner morning would come. She could hardly wait for the moment when Logan would walk through those lobby doors!

If the morning had dragged, the first half of the afternoon seemed even longer. By two o'clock, Gemma was ready and waiting in the pink suit. She had to force herself not to go downstairs right away. There was no point in sitting around in the lobby when Logan had gone to the trouble of arranging for her to keep the room until three. Instead she ordered coffee through room service, and spent an unending forty minutes or so flicking through a copy of the London magazine taken from the writing desk drawer.

At ten minutes to the hour, she took the leather suitcase and her grey handbag and left the room, striding out along the corridor to the lifts with a light heart and a spring in her step. Right here was where the actual audition started. The impression she made on Logan this weekend could well see the beginning of a whole new stage in her career.

By twenty past three, with still no sign of him, she was beginning to feel a little desperate. Supposing he had changed his mind? Supposing he had asked that woman last night to play the part he had offered her—or even maybe settled for a permanent arrangement? They had certainly seemed very close.

Where would that leave her? she wondered dismally. Out in the cold with egg on her face, to mix a couple of metaphors. A suitcase full of new clothes might be considered an adequate enough return for services no longer required, but surely he wouldn't just leave her sitting here like this? If he did he was going to find himself on the receiving end of a very nasty letter. Or would a telephone call make more impression? His private number was ex-directory because she had looked for it, but there was a business number in the book.

She knew she would do no such thing. It would be cutting her own throat. If Logan Telford let her down she had to grin and bear it, and hope he would be grateful enough to grant her the compensation of an audition anyway when she did contact him. Telling him she was an actress might be difficult in the circumstances, but then it would be difficult in any circumstances. Deception created problems.

The sight of the tall, well-built figure coming through the doors inspired mixed emotions, of which relief was not the strongest. She got to her feet as his gaze roved the area, smiling a greeting when their glances clashed, and feeling an inward glow of satisfaction at the sudden recognition in his expression.

'Hallo,' he said. 'Did you enjoy the show last night? You seemed——' He broke off abruptly, eyes narrowing in swiftly assimilated shock. 'Gemma?'

On his lips her name sounded different; she remembered thinking that yesterday when he had repeated it after her in the car coming here. It was the use of the soft G, she thought irrelevantly now. A soft G from a hard man. The contradiction made her tremor inwardly.

'Do you like the new me?' she asked. 'I warn you, it cost the earth!'

'Worth every penny,' he said. 'You look— indescribable!' His smile weakened her at the knees. 'I have the utmost faith in Sally's abilities, but I never realised she was a fairy godmother!'

Gemma laughed. 'I've already got through one midnight without changing back, so I should be safe enough. I thought you weren't coming.'

'Traffic,' he explained succinctly. 'Speaking of which, we'd better be on our way. Just the one suitcase?'

'Isn't it enough for two nights?'

'Depends entirely on viewpoint. I've known women who couldn't travel to the end of the street without taking their whole wardrobe.'

'This *is* my whole wardrobe,' she pointed out. 'Paid for by you, incidentally.' She hesitated. 'I hope Sally didn't spend too much.'

'I told her to spend what was necessary. She'll have done just that.' He hoisted the leather case in one hand, sliding his other under her elbow to turn her towards the doors. 'What did you do with your own clothes?'

'I left them with Sally for the weekend. I might need them later.'

'Why?' he asked. 'From what I saw of them, they didn't have a lot more life left—unless you were carrying a whole lot more than you appeared to be in that rucksack of yours.'

'Only another pair of jeans and some tee-shirts and things,' Gemma admitted, refusing to feel embarrassed about it. 'I haven't had much money to spare for new clothes lately.' Which was true enough, if rather unfair on her mother. The very thought of her mother elicited guilt. That was something else she was going go have to explain sometime, should things to the way she so desperately wanted them to. Only not until she had made a niche for herself in her own name. Now, more than ever, she needed her independence.

The Mercedes was parked on a meter some couple of streets away. Gemma could see the ticket pinned beneath the windscreen wiper as they approached. The sight seemed to bother Logan not a whit. He simply put the suitcase in the boot alongside his own, then settled Gemma in her seat before going round the front to remove the piece of paper in passing.

'I didn't have any small change,' he said by way of explanation as he slid behind the wheel. 'Stuff that in the glove compartment, will you? There's probably one or two there already.'

There was more like half a dozen. Gemma wondered if he ever paid them. Most people doing business in London used taxis or mini-cabs for the very reason that parking was so difficult. Trust Logan to be different!

'How far are we going?' she asked as he put the car into motion and pulled away from the kerb.

'Sevenoaks. We'll be there in time for tea, with any luck. Know it?'

Gemma shook her head, attention captured by a huge pantechnicon coming up on their left-hand side. 'We lived in Tunbridge Wells for a short time when I was small, but I don't remember the area.'

'How long is it since your parents were divorced?'

'Five years.' She was facing front again, trying to sound matter-of-fact about it. 'I thought that thing was going to come right through us!'

There was a pause before he spoke again. 'Still not prepared to talk about it?'

'No.' She made an effort to soften the bare negative. 'It's a rather painful subject. Do you mind?'

'Naturally not. It's your own business. Sometimes it helps to get things off your chest, that's all.' He glanced her way briefly. 'On the other hand, you're probably right. You hardly know me well enough to trust me with confidences.'

But she would like to, Gemma acknowledged silently. How she would like to! The more she saw of Logan Telford the more she knew herself attracted the way she had never been attracted before. It was more than just his looks, more even than what he was. Maturity was the word. Here was a man who was fully adult, so unlike the youths she had hitherto known. The memory of yesterday's little episode made her skin tingle even now. That quality of ruthlessness about him was a part of his magnetism. He would stop at nothing should the mood move him. She wanted to feel his mouth on hers again, his hands on her body. If only they could have met in other circumstances!

They were free of the worst of the city traffic when Logan brought the car to a halt at the roadside, reaching into an inside pocket to take out a small jeweller's box.

'You'd better put this on before we get there,' he said, opening it. 'I took it out on approval. Sale or return. Hope it's the right size. I had to make a guess.'

Gemma reached in with unsteady fingers and extracted the superb diamond solitaire, holding it gingerly between finger and thumb. 'Suppose I lose it?'

'It's well insured.' He sounded amused. 'You don't think they'd have let me bring it out without, do you? Just put it on.'

She did so, feeling a complete fraud. It fitted, if just a little tightly. A shaft of weak sunlight caught the stone, making it sparkle with colour. It was the loveliest piece of jewellery she had ever worn—certainly the most expensive.

'It's beautiful,' she said, 'but I wish I didn't have to wear it.'

'Unfortunately, an engagement without a ring is less than convincing,' he came back on a dry note. 'It suits the new you a lot better than it would done the old.' There was a pause as he looked at her, the expression in his eyes hard to define. Gemma had the feeling he was about to add something else, then he apparently changed his mind, shrugging broad shoulders. 'It will sort itself out,' he said cryptically.

The house was some couple of miles outside the town, standing in its own grounds in the pleasantly wooded Kentish countryside. They were admitted by a maid, and taken straight through to a spacious and beautifully furnished drawing room overlooking the rain-sodden lawns.

Robert and Caryn Powell were both in residence, the latter presiding over a tea-trolley. Meeting the lovely if cool blue eyes of the other woman, Gemma felt shock grip her by the throat. So that was it. Why on earth hadn't Logan warned her! She could feel his presence now at her side, although he wasn't touching her in any way. She couldn't look at him, acknowledging the introductions in a voice that sounded wooden to her ears.

'I'd have expected Logan Telford to pick himself a looker,' stated Robert smilingly in a muted Northern accent. 'About time he got himself spliced!'

'You're only saying that because you finally got yourself trapped,' laughed his wife, taking his arm in a manner Gemma found wholly sickening considering what she knew. 'I hope you'll excuse us starting tea without you. We weren't sure what time you'd be here.' The glance resting on Gemma held a curious expression, almost of anger. 'Did you want to wash your hands before you settle down?'

'That's all right,' Gemma replied, being deliberately obtuse. 'The journey wasn't long enough to get them dirty.' She ignored Logan's sharp look, expression under control. Whatever he got he had asked for. She was nobody's dupe!

Robert invited her to a seat on the chesterfield alongside himself. He was a handsome, well-preserved man in his mid-fifties, his thinning hair shot through with grey. From Logan, she already knew he was an industrialist, and wealthy enough to have opted for early retirement on his marriage. She wondered cynically if Caryn appreciated that retirement, which must to a certain extent limit her own activities. Not that it appeared to have made very much difference last night. The temptation to drop both her and Logan right in it was strong, except that she knew sourgrapes had a lot to do with what she was feeling right now. A little subtle torment wouldn't go amiss, however. They deserved it!

Bringing the conversation around to the theatre wasn't difficult, considering Logan's interests. She waited the appropriate moment with calculation.

'We saw *Cats* last night,' she said brightly. 'A wonderful show!' Her gaze moved from Robert to Caryn, innocent as the day. 'If you haven't already seen it yourselves, you should. I'm sure you'd enjoy it as much as we did.'

This time there was no doubting the emotion expressed in the blue eyes: panic, pure and simple. Gemma would not have been human had she not felt a certain glow of malicious satisfaction, but it was swiftly followed by a faint shame. Playing that kind of game only brought her down to their level. What she had to do was face Logan with his own duplicity and then tell him where he got off! There was no way she was going to spend the weekend aiding and abetting the deception of a man she already found so likeable.

It was Logan himself who seized the initiative, however, walking unannounced into the room to which she had been shown, while she was still in the process of admiring the adjoining bathroom.

'What was all that about downstairs?' he demanded, closing the outer door firmly behind him and standing against it. The grey eyes were cold. 'I don't like innuendo!'

'Not, at any rate, from hired hands,' Gemma came back with level intonation. 'You should have warned me about the set-up. Not that I'd have accepted if you had. I thought this was purely in the interests of business?'

'So it is.'

'Really?' She made no attempt to conceal sarcasm. 'You mean you believe in combining the two?'

His mouth tautened anew. 'My motives are my own concern.'

'No, they're not. Not if you want my help to fulfil them.'

He gazed at her for several seconds in silence, jaw set 'How old did you say you were?' he asked at length.

'Twenty-two.' She lifted an eyebrow in faithful imitation of his own habit. 'Does it make any difference?'

'Not a lot,' he admitted. 'You seem older sometimes than others, that's all.'

Patchy performance, thought Gemma fleetingly. She would have to watch that. Logan was no fool. If he should guess she was putting on an act he might very well begin to suspect her motives.

'I'm not condemning what you do with your private life,' she said. 'That's your—affair.' Jibing at him in that fashion was piling it on a little too much, yet she couldn't stop herself. A man fond of many women, she might have thought him; playing around with another man's wife behind his back while planning to relieve him of a large sum of money was something else again. 'All I am saying is that for this weekend at least you should keep your libido under lock and key and concentrate on the job in hand.'

There was another pause while he studied her, this time with a gradually dawning amusement. 'You know,' he said, 'if the girl I met yesterday had spoken to me like that I'd have put her across my knee. You——'

He moved with deliberation, crossing the room to where she stood by the bathroom door. Gemma made no attempt to resist as he pulled her into his arms, conscious of the fact that she had wanted this very kind of action. The kiss began as a chastisement, but she refused to accept it as such, sliding her arms about his neck to respond with abandonment, sensing his surprise and swift reaction with an inner exultation. Caryn Powell wasn't the only one capable of attracting a man like Logan. She would prove it to her!

The hand sliding inside her blouse had a wonderful familiarity about it. She shivered with pleasure as he teased one hardened nipple between finger and thumb, pressing herself closer to the hard, muscular body. He was kissing her now with soft biting motions of teeth and lips, driving her wild with the sheer frustration of his control.

She felt deprived when he lifted his head, looking into the grey eyes without trying to conceal the desire in hers.

'You're a bundle of surprises,' he said. 'Yesterday I thought you were just another young know-it-all in need of the short, sharp shock treatment. Today——' He paused, glancing down to her opened blouse and the firm, uptilted breast he still held cupped in his hand, a smile curving his lips. 'Today, you're all woman! I appreciate the change.'

'Are you going to take advantage of it?' Gemma asked in the same semi-serious tones, and he laughed.

'Now?'

Every instinct in her cried out to say yes. It took an effort to shake her head and smile in the manner of the character she was playing. 'Well, perhaps not. After all, you have other interests at stake.'

He didn't try to stop her from moving away, leaning against the doorjamb with unreadable expression to watch her button her blouse again. Gemma found her fingers trembling a little as she did so, her nerve beginning to go as she emerged from the part. She had known herself a competent actress prior to this but had never really had the opportunity to prove it quite so devastatingly. Yet it hadn't all been acting, had it? She had wanted Logan to make love to her; she still wanted it. Only if it happened at all it wouldn't be the real Gemma Holt he was taking, just a figment of imagination. He would have no interest in her ordinary everyday self.

'I think you were right,' he said unexpectedly. 'I do owe you some explanation about last night. The problem with Caryn is she finds it next to impossible to let go of anything easily. She and I were together for a few months—very enjoyable months, I might add, but all good things come to an end eventually. Robert came along at the right moment for us both. He's crazy about her. Enough to to give her anything she asks for or shows an interest in.' He paused, mouth suddenly wry. 'With that kind of influence, it's essential to have her on my side when it comes to convincing him about backing the show!'

'Even if it means running the risk of him finding out that the two of you are double-crossing him?' she asked, and saw the wryness give way to impatience.

'You sound like a second-rate film script! If keeping Caryn sweet helps get that backing, I don't give a damn.'

'It depends how far you have to go to do it.' Gemma was speaking from a purely personal viewpoint, allowing her emotions to take over. 'If you're sleeping with her, I don't think you deserve to get your precious backing!'

His eyes had a dangerous glitter. 'Whether I'm sleeping with her or not has nothing to do with you. You're here to do a job, remember? I'll give you the money in advance if it will help you to do just that.'

Gemma looked at him steadily. 'Suppose I told you to keep your money? You can't make me stay.'

'No,' Logan agreed after a moment, without change of inflection, 'I can't. But you'll stay.'

She held his gaze for several seconds before letting hers drop. Walking out now was beyond her, and she knew it. Her attraction to Logan aside, she had too much at stake. 'All right,' she said, 'I'll stick to the bargain we made. Only don't expect *me* to butter Caryn up too.'

It was touch and go, but he let the insinuation pass. 'The act is for Robert. Caryn knows why you're here.'

Gemma wouldn't have been at all surprised if the idea had been Caryn's to start with. Not that her appearance seemed to please the other woman too much. There was the distinct possibility that some approach would be made before the day was out to make sure she knew her place in the scheme of things. That should prove an interesting confrontation.

CHAPTER THREE

THERE were several other invited guests at dinner that evening. Gemma found herself placed next to a man of around Robert's age whose sole topic of conversation was centred on his experiences in bee-keeping. Common courtesy kept a smile on her lips and provided the occasional bright response, but without Robert's frequent if necessarily brief intervention from her other side, she felt she might well have died of boredom long before the meal was through. Catching Caryn's eye at one point, she formed the suspicion that the table placings had been arranged deliberately—at least with regard to her left-hand partner. It gave her incentive to listen to the man with an even greater show of interest the next time he captured her attention.

Coffee and liqueurs were served through in the drawing room. Seated alongside Robert on one of the sofas, Gemma cradled her brandy glass and tried to ignore the fact that Logan and Caryn were *tête-à-tête* in adjoining chairs on the far side of the room. Singling themselves out that way was asking for trouble. Didn't they have the sense to realise that much?

That Robert had also observed the intimate pairing was made evident when he said levelly, 'You knew my wife and your fiancé were acquainted before our marriage, of course?'

'Yes,' Gemma admitted, wondering just how

much Robert himself knew of that relationship.
'Logan told me.'

'Did he tell you they lived together for three
months?' He shook his head at the expression in
her eyes, smiling a little. 'I don't like being at a
disadvantage, either in business or in private life.
At twenty-eight, Caryn was far too beautiful a
woman not to have had other men in her past.'

'Does she realise you know?'

'I doubt it. She apparently believed it might
put me off.'

'But it didn't.'

'As you see. It was over when we met, to all
intents and purposes. She left him less than a
week later.'

Because she had wanted to go, Gemma
wondered, or because Logan had made it all too
plain that there was no secure future with him?
From what he had said this afternoon, the latter
seemed more likely. If he could do that after
three months, what chance did any woman have
of reaching his inner emotions?

'I had an idea it was like that,' she said,
shutting off the depression that thought elicited,
'I wouldn't expect a man of thirty-four to have
lived like a monk.'

'Providing he stays faithful from now on, eh?'
The tone was light but his eyes were serious.
'Trust is an important part of any relationship
between a man and a woman. Logan asked *you* to
marry him. You don't have to be jealous of
Caryn.'

Gemma bit her lip. Did it show so clearly? The
irony of it was that she had no right to feel
anything. Logan had kissed her, that was all.

Given the opportunity, he might well go a great deal further than that, only it wouldn't mean a lot to him. She was just another female so far as he was concerned—with the slight advantage of being of use to him in this one respect. A male chauvinist certainly, yet that label failed to detract from his appeal.

'If you'll take a spot of advice from a man old enough to be your father,' Robert continued on the same light note, 'you'll make very sure he doesn't have need of other women. We're a simple species, on the whole. Satisfy our baser instincts and we lose the desire to stray. After all, who needs to go on searching when the treasure's already been found?'

Gemma was laughing. 'I don't think you're the cynic you're making yourself out to be!'

'No?' His eyes twinkled. 'When you get to know me better you may change your mind. How did you meet Logan?'

Here it was: the question she had been dreading. Gemma felt sick over deceiving this man, yet what other choice did she have now? The time for truth was long past. She trotted out the agreed story in as few words as possible, defending herself against any further enquiry into her background by the time-honoured process of direct attack on another flank.

'Are you going to back the show?' she asked candidly.

Robert looked amused. 'Straight and to the point! I'm used to the roundabout approach.'

'From Logan too?'

'No, but I thought he was the exception. Is he training you, or are you always as unequivocal?'

'I don't see any point in beating about the bush,' Gemma acknowledged. 'I shouldn't have imagined you did either.'

'Meaning it's about time I came out and said which way I'm going to go?' He pursed his lips, looking down into his brandy glass with a thoughtful expression. 'It isn't that simple a decision. I backed his last production and lost a packet.'

'His first failure.'

'Maybe. But *Kiss Me, Kate* isn't a sure-fire winner. He could come another cropper.'

'It would surely depend to a great extent on the casting.' She tried to sound casual about it. 'Most of the vocal numbers go to the leads, of course, but the dancing is vital too.'

His eyes held surprise. 'I didn't realise you were knowledgeable about theatre.'

'I'm not.' Not in that way, she added mentally, excusing the lie. 'I'm—interested, that's all.'

'Enough to have made a study of the whole show.' He was nodding, obviously approving. 'Not only beautiful but bright too. Logan's a lucky man!'

'He doesn't know I've been studying it,' Gemma disclaimed hurriedly, seeing the difficulties lying ahead. 'I'd as soon he didn't.'

'Why on earth not?' He sounded puzzled. 'Surely he'd be only too——' He paused there, enlightenment suddenly dawning. 'You mean he wouldn't appreciate you taking any kind of hand in his business?'

'Something like that,' she murmured.

'Well, I can understand that kind of attitude. I wouldn't have liked it myself. All the same, I can't think he'd be in any way put out because you read up on a few details.'

Suspicion was more what she was afraid of, although she could hardly tell Robert that. So far as Logan would be concerned, she hadn't had time to read up on any detail since meeting him. Should Robert mention this conversation to him, he might just start wondering.

The evening moved on. Conversing with other guests, Gemma gathered the impression that though Robert was well thought of in his circle there were reservations with regard to his choice of a wife. The difference in ages appeared to be the main concern. 'He's worth a vast amount of money, you know,' confided one woman in hushed tones, totally oblivious to the possibility that Gemma could have been a close personal friend of the Powells'. 'It's a big attraction to a younger woman.'

'He's a very attractive man himself,' Gemma pointed out, refusing to be drawn into that kind of speculation.

'Oh, I'm sure!' The other was over-eager in her agreement, sensing a non-sympathiser with her cause. 'Very attractive! All the same——'

All the same indeed, thought Gemma dryly as someone else broke in on the conversation. If any of these people ever found out about last night, suspicion would be confirmed. If Robert himself ever found out about it, heaven help both Caryn and Logan! She had a feeling his reaction would be swift and merciless.

It was gone eleven before Logan made any effort to seek her company, sliding into a seat on the sofa beside her with a smile that nowhere reached the grey eyes.

'You and Robert were having quite a discussion earlier,' he remarked on a deceptively light note. 'About what?'

'About you, as a matter of fact,' she said, adopting the same tone. 'He was warning me to keep the headaches to a minimum if I wanted to stop you thinking about other women.'

'Good advice, if it mattered.' He wasn't amused. 'What else?'

Gemma leaned back comfortably in her seat, wearing a social smile of her own. 'I'm here as a figurehead,' she said without raising her voice, 'not a reporter. I like Robert; I think he likes me. We talked on that basis.'

'You're here as my employee,' he responded hardily. 'If you want that two hundred you'll stop playing the smart alec!'

If she wanted anything at all she was going to have to watch her step, Gemma conceded with an inward sigh. Her position was fast becoming untenable.

'I think you need me even more than I need the two hundred,' she remarked. 'He hasn't made up his mind yet, if that's what you wanted to know. Once bitten, twice shy, I suppose.'

The lean jaw tightened perceptibly. 'You really got down to it, didn't you?

'I suppose he imagined I already knew. It's understandable he should be cautious.' With great daring, she added, 'He thinks the casting could be vital.'

'Of course the casting is vital, dammit! So is the direction.' He was angry now, and not bothering to conceal it. 'Did you bring the subject up yourself?'

Denial was a waste of time. He only had to ask to prove her a liar. 'Yes,' she admitted.

Logan drew in a breadth. 'Who the devil gave you permission?'

'It never occurred to me that it might be needed.' Gemma turned her head a little to study the granite profile, damping down the effect he had on her pulse rate. 'Logan, you're not being fair. I was trying to help.'

'Then don't. Just be convincing as my fiancee.'

'Of course.' Tongue in cheek, she moved sideways to press her lips swiftly and lightly to his cheek in a gesture anyone watching could only construe as impulsive emotion, remaining close with her mouth only inches from his ear. 'Smile, darling, we're being watched!'

Caryn certainly had her eyes on the pair of them: so did most of the other occupants of the room. There were several indulgent smiles.

Logan turned his head so that he was looking directly into her eyes, the glint in his a threat in itself. 'I'll see you later,' he said softly.

Gemma laughed, carried away by her own characterisation. 'I'll be shaking in my shoes!'

'You won't be wearing any,' he promised.

That should have pulled her up, but it didn't. There was a key to the door of her room. All she had to do was turn it. She laughed again and wrinkled her nose at him mockingly. 'Such confidence!'

'Break it up, you two,' said Robert on an amused note, bringing across a decanter. 'Logan, let me give you a refill. After all, you don't have to drive anywhere tonight.'

The other man shook his head, staying right where he was. 'Thanks, but no. I've had enough.'

Robert's glance went from his to Gemma's face with a little smile of comprehension. 'You know your own limit. Who am I to argue!'

If nothing else had succeeded in quieting her, that certainly did. Robert was taking it for granted that they planned on spending the night together, even though they had been allocated separate rooms. But Caryn would have done the allocating, wouldn't she? No doubt Robert would have put them in the same room. How like men were men!

Someone came to sit on Logan's other side on the sofa, drawing him into a discussion on the relative merits of the apron and traditional stage designs. Gemma made her escape on the pretext of going to the bathroom, dodging instead into the library across the hall in order to give herself a little breathing space. If she had gone too far in there, then so had Logan. He would have her asking him for permission to speak at all next!

There was a gilded mirror on the far wall. From where she stood she could see her reflection, lit from behind by the wall-bracket she had switched on. The dress she was wearing was the same creamy colour as her skin, scooped low at the neckline. In the dim light her hair looked jet-black, her eyes as deep as pools beneath the straight slash of the fringe. For a brief moment she actually wished she could go back to being the other Gemma, but only for a moment. Looking like this she could get away with so much more— could dare so much more. Only if this weekend was all she had she was going to have to work very hard at it.

She was still standing there dreaming when Caryn came into the room.

'I thought it might be you in here,' she said from the doorway. 'What are you doing?'

'Thinking,' Gemma responded, pulling herself together. 'Just thinking.'

'Are you sure you don't mean hoping?' The other's voice was tart. 'I'm not sure where Logan picked you up, but he'll be putting you right down again as soon as the weekend is over!'

'Shouldn't that be "as soon as Robert agrees to back the show"?' asked Gemma innocently. 'He may not decide this weekend.'

'He'll decide.' The tone alone was decisive. 'I'll make sure of it!'

Gemma looked back at her calmly. 'If you can. I doubt if your husband is quite the fool you seem to take him for.'

'What would you know about it?'

'Enough to feel sympathy for him. He deserves better. If you prefer Logan you should have stuck to him. Or weren't you given the option?'

Caryn's eyes were glittering. 'You take a little too much on yourself!'

She was probably right about that if nothing else, Gemma was bound to concede. Yet no one could say it was none of her business what this woman and Logan got up to. He had made her a part of his affairs himself. If she took a few liberties he could hardly complain.

'So what do you plan on doing about it?' she asked boldly. 'So far as your husband is concerned, I'm Logan's fiancée. Are you going to tell him different?'

'No, but I'm sure Logan isn't going to take very kindly to your interference.'

'I'll look forward to his—chastisement.' Gemma was being deliberately provocative, wanting to undermine this woman's supreme confidence in her own power. 'He's very good at that, isn't he? I don't blame you for finding him attractive still. Who wouldn't? All the same, I really think you should settle for what you have. Robert's a fine man, and he thinks the sun shines out of you. Why disillusion him?'

'I don't intend to disillusion him.' Caryn said it through her teeth. 'And you'd better not either!'

'I wouldn't hurt him for the world,' Gemma denied. 'But neither would I be in your shoes if he ever finds out that you're still seeing Logan privately.'

It was a moment or two before Caryn could bring herself to reply. She seemed lost for words. 'Damn you!' she snapped viciously in the end. 'You're going to regret this!'

Gemma didn't doubt it. But it had needed saying. She waited two or three minutes after Caryn departed before making her own way back to the drawing room, meeting Logan's questioning glance with a bland expression. He would know soon enough; Caryn would make certain of that. If what he had said in the bedroom earlier was true, then he should be grateful that someone had seen fit to point out what the woman was risking. Influence she might have, but when it came down to investments, Robert Powell stood out a mile as a man who would make his own decisions regardless. It was surprising that Logan himself couldn't see it.

They were the only guests staying the night. Robert suggested a nightcap after the last of the others had departed, accepting Gemma's plea of tiredness with good grace.

'They're forecasting a dry day tomorrow,' he said before she took her leave. 'It could even be warm enough for a swim. We've had the cover on the pool for the past two weeks. If you didn't bring a suit I'm sure Caryn can find you one.' He took his wife's agreement for granted, his smile purely for Gemma. 'Goodnight, my dear. I'm glad Logan had the good sense to put you under contract!'

The choice of words was ironic. Gemma kept her expression strictly controlled as she made her escape. In her role as loving fiancée, she had intended kissing Logan goodnight, but the glint in his eyes deterred her. She was going to have enough to answer for in the morning as it was.

The bedside lamps were already on in her room, the sheets turned invitingly back. The maid had extracted her slinky black satin nightdress from the drawer where she had put it, and laid it across the pillow. Sally had insisted on that particular purchase, perhaps also reading more into this weekend with Logan than existed. Sliding into it, Gemma felt the sheer sensuality of the material stir her senses. A pity it was going to be wasted, but wasted it was going to be. There was no future in wanting Logan Telford the way she did undoubtedly want him. He would simply take anything she had to offer and go on his way untouched.

It was only when she went to lock the door that she discovered the key was missing. A search of the floor area in the immediate vicinity failed to reveal it, which left her with the one alternative: someone had deliberately removed it.

The maid seemed unlikely, so it had to be Logan. Standing there looking at the empty keyhole, Gemma tried to conjure anger and indignation, but the rapid beating of her heart had little to do with either emotion. He had said he would see her later, only she hadn't taken him seriously enough. The problem was what to do now?

So far as she could see it, she had two choices: she could either put on a wrap and go back downstairs to ask one of the three staff members for another key—causing speculation to run amok, to say the least—or she could simply wait for Logan to come, and show him exactly where he stood so far as she was concerned. The latter course was really the only choice in the long run, although the danger was obvious. Suppose he refused to take no for an answer?

So make him, she told herself firmly. A man like Logan would never stoop to force; not even where he felt himself safe from accusation. Yesterday had been a totally different situation.

She left a light burning purposely, lying on her back in the very centre of the double bed with her arms neatly by her sides over the top of the bedding. Laid out for sacrifice, she thought with a flash of humour. Honestly, this was becoming ridiculous! Why didn't she just relax and go to sleep?

The thought alone seemed enough. She awoke again only when the mattress tilted slightly to Logan's weight as he slid in beside her.

'I like the black satin,' he said softly with his mouth close against her ear, 'but you're hardly going to need it.' His hand ran the length of her body, his touch already possessive. 'Your skin is just as smooth as this. That much I've discovered.'

Gemma stiffened as he reached the bottom hem of the garment and began a slow and tantalising movement up the bare length of her leg, forcing a reaction her whole body cried out to reject. The fingers gripping that supple hand were somewhat less than emphatic.

'Get out!' she hissed.

'The next line should be "How dare you!" if that's the way we're playing it,' he responded on a note of amusement. 'I expected a little more originality from you, Gemma. Surely you're not going to disappoint me?'

Despite her hold on it, the hand had already reached her knee. Now his fingers slid round to the back, caressing the soft skin there with a lightness of touch that sent shiver after shiver down her spine. Gemma closed her eyes as his mouth found hers, lips parting of their own accord to the subtle demand. Her loss of control lasted bare seconds. She felt his head jerk as she bit him, and took advantage of his momentary withdrawal to wriggle away from him, kicking away the sheet with the intention of getting up out of the bed.

The arm snaking about her waist was far from gentle. One pull had her on her back again, this time with one of his legs thrown across hers to stop her from moving. His face in the light from the single lamp had a devilish cast.

'That wasn't nice,' he said. 'I'm going to have to teach you some manners!'

'I don't want you to teach me anything!' she gasped, ceasing the futile struggling. 'Logan, stop this! Get out of my room!'

'No way. Not after the way you've acted all day. Was I planning to take advantage, you asked me this afternoon. Well, yes, that's exactly what I'm planning to do.' He was speaking in low but purposeful tones, the faintest of smiles curling the corners of his lips. 'And you're going to know I've taken it!'

Gemma used her free hand to pummel at his shoulder as he sought her lips again, knowing she was simply making a gesture. If she bit him again he would only bite her right back; he had made that perfectly clear. What was she fighting over anyway? She had wanted this earlier, and she wanted it now. So what if there was no future in it? Could that detract from the sensations he was arousing right this minute?

She heard him make a small sound of satisfaction as she relaxed beneath him, but was too far gone to care about the so-called ignominy of admitting defeat. Her arms slid about him, holding him closer, her lips answering his in the same hungering vein. He had shaved before coming to her; the smoothness of his jawline told her that much. The faint tangy scent of his skin made her nostrils tingle, filling her head with a craving she couldn't assuage alone.

Her kisses grew feverish, her body moving against him without restraint. Later she would remember the expertise with which he removed the satin nightdress; for now she was concerned only

with the feel of his hands on her skin, with the
emotions running riot inside her. There was a brief
moment when he drew away to remove the silk
dressing gown that was his only covering, then he
was back with her, body hard and assertive,
compelling her to yield to him, his weight
suspended above her as he took her with him to
heights she had only barely anticipated, collapsing
at that final, engulfing moment when Gemma
herself could no longer withstand the need to let go.

Logan was the first to recover, rolling to one
side to relieve her of his weight but leaving an
arm about her, hand at her breast.

'Still full of surprises!' he murmured. He put
his lips to her temple where the hair clung
damply. 'That was worth repeating!'

Gemma stirred beneath the warm heaviness of
the arm pinning her so securely in place. What
she felt at this precise moment she wasn't wholly
sure: all she did know was that physical repletion
only went so far.

'This wasn't supposed to happen,' she said
huskily. 'Yesterday morning I didn't even know
you!'

'The morning before that, actually,' he corrected, smiling a little. 'It's almost two o'clock.'

She moved her head on the pillow, trying not
to let him guess her mental turmoil. 'Don't be
facetious about it! You know what I mean.'

'I know what I think you mean. I can't see
what difference it makes. It had to happen some
time. We both knew that.'

'Sooner rather than later, considering the limit
on our time together?' she suggested, and sensed
the inner shrug.

'If you like. Once this weekend is over we each go our own way, remember?'

'I remember.' Gemma controlled her voice by sheer willpower. 'When you offered me the two hundred pounds did you have this in mind too?'

The indrawn hiss of his breath sounded loud in the silence of the room. He came up on an elbow, taking his hand from her breast to seize her by the chin and turn her face towards him. The grey eyes were dangerous. 'One more crack like that one and I'll be giving you something else to remember me by!' he threatened. 'I'm not in the habit of paying for a woman!'

Gemma could imagine. No doubt he could pick and choose from a whole queue. She refused to flinch away from the hard regard. 'You're right, that was uncalled for. I'm sorry.'

For a moment he was still, searching her eyes as if suspecting a certain lack of sincerity, then he relaxed again. 'Okay, forget it.' His gaze dropped to her mouth, taking on a new expression. 'I want you again, Gemma.'

'No!' The denial came out sharper than she had intended, lifting his brows in sudden sardonic enquiry.

'Why not? Is once enough for you?'

'Yes. I mean——' She stopped abruptly, conscious of her own inadequacy to explain. His arm had returned to its previous position, holding her down until he chose to let her go. 'Logan, let's just call it a day,' she begged. 'I'm not cut out for this.'.

'That's not the impression you gave me a few minutes ago.' He put his lips to the curve of her jaw, moving them slowly and tantalisingly along the smooth line until he reached her lobe, then using the tip of his tongue to rouse her to quivering response. 'Now, try telling me you don't want me again,' he whispered. 'You're as ready as I am!'

It was useless denying it when her body made a liar of her. Too late now anyway, she acknowledged fatalistically. She should have refused the first time. He would have accepted it if she'd been emphatic enough.

He took it slowly this time, making her wait his pleasure. There was a wealth of experience and knowledge in those hands of his, their every touch calculated to drive her closer to the edge. Gemma was helpless to stop the gathering storm inside her; helpless to do anything but follow his lead. When he took her it was like an explosion; she heard her own voice cry out through the tumult.

She came awake at dawn when he got out of the bed, watching him reach for and pull on the thin silk robe with numb acceptance. She made no pretence of being asleep when he turned his head to look down at her.

'Hi!' he said softly. 'It seems Robert might be right about the weather. It's going to be fine.'

Damn the weather! she thought. If the sun shone from now till Christmas it couldn't alter circumstances. This afternoon they would travel back to town, and there they would part. Interlude over. After last night she could never bring herself to ask for that audition. Logan would believe she had only given herself to him with that sole purpose in mind.

Kneeling on the mattress edge, he bent to kiss

her, mouth unexpectedly tender. 'You've made this weekend something special,' he said. 'Do you know that?'

It took every ounce of willpower she possessed to stop herself from revealing the true state of her emotions at that moment. 'I'll take your word for it,' she said. 'See you at breakfast.'

He remained where he was for a second or two, head on one side as he studied her, and an odd expression in his eyes, then he shrugged and pushed himself to his feet. 'Sure.'

Gemma lay motionless until the door had closed quietly behind him. She felt crushed and heartsick. One night's pleasure was all she was going to have to remember him by. Had it been worth it?

CHAPTER FOUR

THE sun was shining when Gemma opened her eyes again. Her watch said seven-thirty. She got out of bed immediately, averting her eyes from the discarded nightdress on the floor. She would pack it away as soon as she had taken a shower. For the present she didn't even want to think about the happenings of the night.

The latter course was impossible, of course. She had to think about it. In another hour or so she would be seeing Logan across the breakfast table, and by then she had to be fully in command of her reactions. It wouldn't do to have him guess how she was feeling. Commitments were the last thing he sought.

Fancying herself in love with him would be ridiculous, she reflected. One couldn't love a man one barely knew. What they had shared last night was a purely physical experience, albeit a wonderful one. Regardless of what happened now, she couldn't bring herself to regret it.

Angling for an audition was still out of the question. Even to tell him the truth about her background now would cause the same misunderstandings. Let him go on believing she was what she had pretended to be—that way she at least retained some pride in herself.

Dressed in cotton slacks and thin pink shirt, she made her way downstairs, smiling a greeting to the maid mounting with a tray set for one.

'Mr Powell is out by the pool,' advised the latter. 'It's a lovely morning, miss!'

'Beautiful,' Gemma agreed. 'How do I get out to the pool?'

'Through the library would be the shortest way.' The girl smiled again and continued on her way.

Last night the curtains had been drawn across the library wall. This morning they stood back to reveal french doors leading out on to the side of the house, Robert was sitting at a wrought iron table already set with places for three, a newspaper opened in front of him.

'You're an early bird,' he greeted her. 'Caryn never puts in an appearance before eleven on a Sunday. Do you want to eat right away, or start out with juice American style?'

'The juice sounds good.' Gemma slipped into a seat opposite, eyes skimming the oval pool a few feet away before coming back to her host. The dampness of his hair told its own story. 'How's the water?'

'Comfortable,' he said. 'It should be—I keep it heated to seventy degrees.'

She laughed. 'Where's your British fortitude!'

'Abandoned,' he admitted, grinning back. 'I'm a luxury-lover, and proud of it! Why don't you see if there's a spare suit that will fit you in one of the cabins over there,' indicating the latter with a movement of his head. 'There's usually a couple around in case of unexpected visitors. Tone you up for the day!'

A swim would be nice, Gemma conceded. She got up and walked the few yards to the small cabins built behind a section of trellis overflowing with freesia. The first was empty apart from a wooden bench seat. a slatted draining board and a couple of hooks, but the second of the two had no fewer than three bikinis slung by their straps. The blue patterned one looked roughly her size. She undressed swiftly and got into it, stepping outside again to the delicious warmth of the sun on her bare skin.

'Fast,' approved Robert. 'Not that it wouldn't have been worth waiting for!' He was looking at her with unconcealed appreciation. 'Does that hairstyle take to water?'

'I don't know,' Gemma admitted. 'I haven't had it long enough to find out.'

She gave him a wide white smile and ran past him to dive smoothly and shallowly into the pool, skimming along beneath the surface for the full length before surfacing. Holding on to the side rim, she shook her head to lose excess moisture, feeling her hair fall heavily and naturally back into place.

'It works,' observed Robert, watching her from his seat. 'Good. I'd have hated you to spoil that Cleopatra image of yours!'

She would give lot a for the same power, Gemma acknowledged ruefully. Except that Logan was no Antony. When it came down to a choice between work and a woman, the former would certainly win.

Her orange juice was waiting, along with a huge fluffy towel, when she eventually decided she had had enough. Robert held the towel out for her as she climbed from the pool, wrapping it about her shoulders with solicitous concern. Logan came out from the house while he was doing it, his regard sardonic.

'Having fun?' he inquired.

Robert laughed, making no attempt to move away in a hurry. 'Caught in the act, eh? Can you blame me?'

'Not one iota.' Grey eyes held green, expression unchanged. 'She's a fetching piece.'

'She had to be to land you.' Robert regained his seat, leaving Gemma to finish towelling herself dry on the pool edge. 'When's the wedding to be?'

It was Logan's turn to laugh. 'Give it a chance!'

'Three months is more than a chance. I left it a bit late to start thinking about having kids, but you're still inside the limit—always providing you get on with it pretty soon, that is.'

It was Gemma who answered that one, coming over to join the two men. 'We don't plan on having any children,' she said smoothly. 'They'd interfere with our lifestyle.'

Robert looked at her for a long moment with suddenly narrowed eyes. 'I might believe that from Logan, but you don't strike me as the materialistic type.'

'Which just goes to prove how deceptive looks can be.' Logan sounded easy enough, but the hardness of his jawline betrayed him. 'It will happen when it happens. You'll be kept advised.'

'We'd better be.' Robert's tone was also easy. 'I'm sure Caryn wouldn't want to miss the occasion. Women do love a wedding.' The pause was brief but pointed. 'Thinking of having a swim before breakfast?'

Logan shook his head, eyes travelling the length of Gemma's bare legs as she sat down at the table, and on up to her face. The quirk of one dark brow was reminder enough. She made herself return the gaze without flinching. There was no way he was going to get through her guard.

'Are we going to do some talking this morning?' he asked bluntly, turning his attention back to their host. 'Or was this weekend just a softener towards saying no?'

'I haven't decided,' Robert admitted, unmoved by the frontal attack. 'And I don't intend to in a hurry. I'll need to know more about production costs first.'

'Sure.' If Logan was frustrated by the delaying tactics he wasn't showing it. Propping one calf comfortably across the other knee, he added, 'It's going to take a day or two to get it together.'

The other nodded. 'Naturally. Which brings me to another suggestion. I've leased Bray-Simpson's yacht for a couple of weeks starting Wednesday. Why don't you and Gemma join us, then we can get down to business with plenty of time to spare?' He switched his glance to Gemma. 'You'd like a cruise round the Greek islands, wouldn't you?'

'I can't spare a couple of weeks,' put in Logan hardily before she could answer. 'Stop stalling, man!'

The older man ignored the injunction. 'A week then, or even a few days. We're flying out Wednesday. You could take a flight Friday and stay till—whenever. Do you both good to get some sea air.'

Gemma choked over the orange juice, turning it into a cough as both men looked at her. 'Sorry,' she spluttered, 'it went down the wrong way.'

Logan eyed her thoughtfully for a moment before returning to the subject in hand. 'Are you making it a condition?'

'Let's just say I'd prefer the time and place.' Robert was obviously a man accustomed to getting his own way; it showed in the very manner with which he dismissed the whole topic as settled. 'The boat's docked at Piraeus. We'll probably have the crew take her out for a short run along the coast over Thursday, but we'll be back in plenty of time to pick you up.'

Gemma waited for Logan's refusal, glancing at him with a question in her eyes when it failed to materialise. He met the look expressionlessly.

So what now? she wondered. It was hardly possible that he was going to ask her to accompany him on that kind of trip, although the thought of it alone filled her with longing. Yet it was also obvious that Robert was not going to be pushed into making the decision until he was good and ready. Logan must need him badly to stay the course.

The maid came out to see if they were ready to order breakfast yet. Gemma asked for toast and coffee, and took advantage of the preparation time to go and dress. Logan was sitting alone when she got back, one arm resting along the table top as he gazed out across the pool. The short-sleeved cotton shirt revealed muscular biceps and skin tanned to a shade of bronze he could never have acquired in England—at least not this summer. The memory of what it felt like to be in those arms shortened her breath.

'Telephone,' he said succinctly before she could ask what had happened to Robert. 'He'll be back.' He turned his head as she sat down, expression difficult to read. 'How *do* you feel about a trip to the Greek islands?'

Gemma stared at him without answering for several seconds, unable to accept that he might be serious. 'It isn't on, is it?' she said at last. 'I'm surprised you don't call it a day where Robert's concerned, and find another backer, or backers, as the case might be.'

'As simple as that?' His lips twisted. 'In this day and age they don't exactly pop out of the woodwork.'

'So take the risk yourself.' Her tone was deliberately flippant. 'That way you don't have to go cap in hand to anyone.'

'I've already taken on a fair percentage. I can hardly carry the whole load.'

'Why?' she taunted. 'Scared of another flop?' It didn't need his sudden change of expression to tell her she had gone too far; she was regretting the jibe even as she made it. An apology was called for, but the word refused to come.

'Why the aggro?' he asked bitingly. 'Last night was a joint venture. If you had any complaints you should have made them then.'

Her shrug was defensive. 'Who's complaining? I'm sure a thousand women would give their all to be where I was last night!'

'If you want to take another swim, just keep that line up.' Although he hadn't moved, the very tone was warning enough. 'Just try being consistent, will you? Right now you're acting like a sixteen-year-old!'

'For all you know, that's all I might be,' Gemma retorted, stung. She laughed at the look in the grey eyes, enjoying the momentary power. 'It would still be legal, don't worry!'

Logan moved then, so swiftly she didn't have time to evade his reaching hand. Swinging her up from the floor, he walked over to the pool and tossed her in. By the time she came spluttering to the surface, he was back in his seat at the table and smiling unconcernedly at the maid as she deposited a tray.

Robert reappeared as Gemma climbed from the water via the iron ladder. He looked at her for a moment as if she were mad before glancing Logan's way in sudden comprehension.

'Premarital strain?'

'You could say that.' Logan didn't even bother to turn his head in Gemma's direction. 'We'll be joining you on Friday.'

'Good.' Robert sounded amused. 'I wonder who was trying to persuade whom?'

The maid had hastily retreated. Bringing all her control of character to bear, Gemma sat down dripping in the chair from which she had so recently been dragged and reached for a piece of toast.

'Now that,' said Robert admiringly, 'is what I call cool!'

'Warm,' Gemma corrected between bites. 'You keep it at seventy degrees, remember.' She met Logan's eyes with careful aplomb. 'You're so impulsive, darling!'

The grin was as sudden as it was unexpected. 'Now you know what I see in her,' he said to Robert. 'I'm never quite sure what's coming next!'

'That must give life a certain spice.'

The wry note could have been imaginary, Gemma told herself, only she didn't really think so. Robert was perceptive enough to be fully aware that he had been married for his money. Caryn should consider herself fortunate to have found a man who loved her enough to accept that fact.

Only now, with her dignity retrieved, could she begin to think seriously about the immediate future. Logan had not been playing games when he had asked how she felt about the cruise; he had confirmed that much just now. So how did she feel? That was a difficult question to answer. On the one hand was temptation, on the other caution. The longer she spent in Logan's company the harder it was going to be to say goodbye.

Yet how to get out of it now without allowing Robert to suspect something wrong? Her supposed job, perhaps?

'About Friday,' she said. 'I may not be able to get leave at such short notice.'

'That's no problem,' Logan returned imperturbably. 'I'll have a word with Gary myself. I'll even pay for a temp if necessary.'

'Never say die should be your family motto,' said Robert on a dry note, and received a bland half smile.

'It is.'

Gemma flung caution to the winds, acknowledging her desperate need to make this trip. There still remained the question of what she was going to do with herself until Friday, but no doubt Logan would do the arranging. She was going to need more clothes too, and he would have to do the buying; she wasn't supposed to have any money. If he ever found out how she had deceived him there was going to be hell to pay. Gemma didn't want to think about it. Should it happen she would face it then.

And what about professional ambition? asked another part of her mind, only she didn't want to think about that either. In two short days Logan had become the focal point of her world. Getting him out of her system was her first priority.

Her clothing was almost dry in the warmth of the sun by the time they finished breakfast, though too crumpled to continue wearing. Robert followed her indoors when she announced her intention of going up to change, saying he had a phone call to make. Entering the library from this direction, she was looking directly at a framed photograph standing on the mahogany desk set at right angles to the windows. Recognition was instant and devastating, stopping her in her tracks.

'My son Jason,' Robert supplied, following the line of her gaze as he sat down behind the desk and pulled the telephone towards him. 'We're what you might call estranged at the moment.' His hand was on the receiver, but he made no attempt to lift it, looking at the photograph with a rueful expression. 'Three years' theatrical training, and he finishes up dossing down in barns with a group of so-called travelling players!'

'I didn't realise you'd been married before.' Her voice sounded thick in her ears. 'What you said about children out there a few minutes ago——'

'True, so far as it goes. I was only in my mid-thirties when Jason's mother died. If I'd married again sooner, I'd probably have more than one kid to concentrate on now.'

'You're not exactly ancient,' Gemma pointed out, trying to lighten the atmosphere. 'Chaplin was in his seventies.'

'With a wife who wanted a family.' Robert shook his head. 'I knew Caryn didn't want children before I married her. I don't regret anything.' He was still looking at the photograph as he added softly, 'I also know she doesn't feel as much for me as I do for her, but so long as she sticks to her side of the bargain, I can take it.' His eyes moved to her face then, his smile a little wry. 'That's one of the reasons why I want you and Logan to spend some time with us on the boat. The more she sees the two of you together, the more she has to realise that she's wasting her time hankering after him. You're what Logan needs, Gemma—someone he can rely on to back him regardless. I'm not fooled by all this play-acting between the two of you. I think you've assessed him accurately enough to realise how bored he could become with total predictability, and you feel enough for him to make the effort not to be.'

So near and yet so far. It was on the tip of Gemma's tongue to blurt out the truth right there and then, only what good would it do? Logan's motives would come under immediate suspicion, for one thing, to say nothing of her own. She had agreed to this masquerade, she had to go through with it. If it only put a stop to any further deception, it would be worth it.

She made her escape feeling low. Reaching her room, she stripped off the slacks and shirt and took a shower to rid her hair and skin of any chemicals that might have been in the water.

Standing beneath the warm stream, she finally allowed herself to consider the possible implications of what she had learned in the library. Jason Powell, of all people! It was over a year since he had finished his training, and they had never been a part of the same set, yet for a brief period of time they had shared a certain closeness. There had been no reason to connect the name: to be honest with herself, she had almost forgotten Jason had ever existed. The only consolation lay in what Robert had said about his relationship with his only son. It was unlikely in the circumstances that the latter would be joining them on this cruise. Robert would surely have mentioned it had there been any chance at all. She was safe enough, just sorry to discover yet another secret to keep. At this rate she would soon find it difficult to separate the truth from the lies even in her own mind.

Clad only in a towel, she emerged from the bathroom to find Logan standing at the window looking out over the grounds. He turned as she paused in the doorway, regard quizzical.

'Does daylight make a difference?' he asked as she made an involuntary move to tuck the towel more firmly about her. 'I've seen you in less. You could say, so has Robert. That shirt of yours came out of the water practically transparent!'

Gemma stayed where she was, summoning restraint. 'Whose fault was that?'

'Yours for asking for it—and for not wearing something underneath. Not that you need to, I have to admit.' His tone altered a fraction, taking on a note that curled her up inside. 'I don't know about Rob, but my hands were itching to reach out and touch. They still are!'

Gemma licked suddenly dry lips, desisting abruptly as his eyes followed the movement of her tongue. Just a word and a look, and he had her in flames. It would be so easy to just give in to that sweeping desire. Too easy. She wasn't his possession, to come running whenever he beckoned a lean brown finger. That was one thing he had to learn.

'Is that the only reason you're here?' she got out with creditable control.

'No,' he admitted. 'Although I'd have said it was good enough.' The grey eyes were derisive, as aware of her inner response as she was herself. 'Why don't you put some clothes on, and remove the temptation. Then we can talk sensibly.'

The only garments she had not yet worn were a plain, straight skirt and silk shirt in toning greys. She seized them on their hangers from the wardrobe fitment, ignoring his smile at the single garment she pulled from a drawer. She had never worn a brassiere in her life, and didn't intend to start until she was forced by the laws of gravity. Whatever he might think to the contrary, it had nothing to do with sexual equality, just plain and simple freedom of movement. Damn him, she thought viciously at that point, he even had her making excuses for her own behaviour!

He was still in the same place when she came out again. Feeling more selfconscious dressed than she had in the towel, Gemma waited for him to make the first move.

'Sit down,' he invited, indicating the single chair.

'This is my room,' she pointed out. 'You sit down.'

Shrugging, he did so, making her feel petty and childish—which was probably the intention. 'One or two matters we need to discuss,' he said. 'About the coming week——'

'You're taking a little too much for granted.' Although she had already decided to accompany him on the Friday, she was not about to let him off scot free. 'I haven't actually said I'll go yet.'

His face hardened. 'What are you after—more money?'

This time she could not control the run of colour under her skin. Eyes sparking, she said bitingly, 'You can keep your money! It doesn't buy everything!'

'Just most things,' he came back, unmoved by the outburst. He studied her flushed cheeks with cynicism. 'You know, you're a natural! If you ever decide to take up the stage, let me know. I can think of a couple of parts you'd be perfect in!'

If ever there had been a time for telling him the truth that time was now, yet Gemma couldn't bring herself to take advantage of it. 'You're not making this any easier,' she said instead. 'For two pins I'd walk out on you right this very minute!'

'So if it isn't money, what's stopping you?' He wasn't giving an inch. 'Concern for my welfare?'

'More for Robert's,' she retorted, taking a grip on herself. 'He isn't stupid. He knows very well that Caryn still feels something for you. Why else do you imagine he's insisting on pushing your relationship with me down her throat? Why else

would he want us both right there on that boat
with them?'

Logan was looking at her as if he had never
really seen her before, eyes narrowed to the
movement of her lips. 'You know too much for
your own good. Supposing you leave it to me to
keep Caryn at a distance?'

'If that's what you intend doing.'

'That's exactly what I intend doing. Which
brings us right back to where we started. There's
tonight, and four more to get through before
Friday.' The glint warned her against any clever
comments. 'I think it would be a good idea if you
stayed at my place in town rather than a hotel.'

'So you can keep an eye on me?' Gemma asked,
heart thudding against her ribs.

'Among other things.' His smile was intended
to stir her. 'There's only one bedroom.'

'So you're going to sleep on the sofa?'

He laughed at that. 'Very droll! At least you're
never boring, darling.'

She would have fired a heated reply to that
piece of male chauvinism, except that she knew
he was deliberately goading her. The invitation
had been unexpected: she barely knew what
answer to make.

'I'd have thought once was enough of that kind
of arrangement,' she said at length.

His mouth curled briefly. 'Rob certainly did do
some confiding, didn't he?'

'He thought I should know. Unlike some, he
believes people should start out with a clean
slate.'

'You mean he was paying back a few dues.
Don't run away with the idea that Robert Powell

is all heart and honour. He wouldn't be where he is today without a ruthless streak.' He paused, expression undergoing a faint and undefinable change. 'Anyway, Caryn was a different proposition altogether.'

Gemma could imagine. No way was their affair going to last three months. That knowledge alone should have been enough to make up her mind, yet she still found herself hesitating. To say no now would be like closing the door after the horse had bolted. Five days with Logan could very well be worth a whole lifetime of regret!

'Having difficulty?' he asked, watching her. 'Let me make it easier. You don't have anywhere else to go, and I still haven't given you your two hundred.'

'That's blackmail!'

'Persuasion,' he corrected. 'So is this——'.

She said nothing as he took hold of her, nor did she attempt to evade his lips. The kiss woke memories of the night before, rousing her immediately to response. Her breasts felt crushed against the hardness of his chest, but it was a pain she welcomed. Being in Logan's arms again was all the persuasion she needed.

The silk shirt she had so recently donned slipped its buttons easily, sliding from her shoulders to the gentle push of his hands. She quivered as those same fingers found her breasts, cupping them both from beneath while his thumbs teased her nipples into taut peaks of desire.

'Beautiful!' Logan murmured against her lips.

Gemma felt bereft when he put her away from him, her body roused to a pitch of anticipation where fulfilment was all that was left. He was smiling, regret mingled with some other subtle emotion.

'It will keep,' he said. 'Tonight we'll have all the time in the world. I've a feeling we'll both benefit from a little frustration right now.'

She made a supreme effort to match his mood, aware that he was testing her own quality of control. Her smile as she reached for her shirt looked only slightly forced. 'You're right. We should go down and show our faces before lunch. What would Caryn think!'

He had been moving away. Now he paused and looked back at her, face hardening just a fraction. 'Let's leave Caryn out of it, shall we? She's in the past.'

Meaning she had outlived her usefulness. Gemma wondered fleetingly if the other woman was going to be prepared to accept her dismissal quite so easily.

CHAPTER FIVE

THEY left at two-thirty after a luncheon which Gemma for one would as soon have foregone. Driving back to town with the memory of Caryn's parting shot on her mind was no aid to digestion.

'You won't keep him,' the other woman had said, cornering her in the bedroom as she gathered her things prior to the leavetaking. 'You might have managed to talk Robert into inviting you on this Greek trip, but Logan is a different proposition, I can tell you. He'll use you as long as he has need, then dump you just as easily as he picked you up!'

There were several cutting replies Gemma could have made to that, but they would have been no more worthwhile than denying the assumption that she had been the one to suggest her inclusion in the cruise plans. Silence was a much more effective weapon where a woman of Caryn's type was concerned, although it still left her with a nasty taste in her mouth when she thought about those few minutes of invective. It was the truth in what Caryn had said that hurt the most, of course. Logan had no real feeling for her. Once the deal with Robert was sealed, they would return to London and complete their own. Except that there was no way she was going to be taking any money from him now. When the time came, she would simply fade out of his life without a forwarding address.

The flat was in a converted warehouse overlooking the river at Southwark. Walking the length of the huge, divided living area to look out through sliding doors on to a plant-lined patio, Gemma found herself mentally calculating the probable rental for such a place. Financially, Logan had to be very much more than merely solvent to live here—from a personal point of view, at least.

'The kitchen is behind that wooden screen,' he advised as he carried the two weekend cases across to the open-plan staircase on the far side of the room. 'As I said, there's just the one bedroom.'

Gemma visually followed his ascent to the wide loft jutting out from one end of the roof space, able to catch a glimpse of a double bed mounted on a shallow dais towards the rear. Sheer curtaining mounted on ceiling tracks either side of the area formed the only possible means of privacy from below, and that itself would be more illusionary than real. She only hoped the bathroom was more traditionally styled!

'Make yourself at home,' Logan invited, dropping both suitcases to the floor and coming back to the slatted railing to look down at her. 'Don't stand on ceremony. If you want tea, you'll find it in one of the brown canisters. Coffee's next to it.'

'Which would you prefer?' asked Gemma, and saw him grin.

'I'm glad to hear my preferences matter. Coffee for me. Strong and black.'

Gemma went to comply, finding the kitchen area well equipped and organised. An Italian smoked glass table and six comfortably padded chrome chairs stood behind a further partition set at right angles to the first. The display of flowers at the centre of the table looked freshly arranged, until one took a slightly closer scrutiny and realised the whole thing was made from a porcelain so fine as to be almost translucent.

As a *pied-à-terre* the place was ideal, she thought; as a regular home it left a lot to be desired. Not that such matters were going to be of any concern to her. She was here strictly on a temporary basis.

The thought of the coming night made her pulses quicken. Foolish she might be for accepting such a one-sided arrangement in the first place, but having done so there was no way she was going to waste time in regrets. She had one, maybe two weeks with Logan, and she was going to live every minute. When the time came to part, then she would accept that too. One had to pay a price for everything.

Logan was on the telephone when she took the coffee through to the main living area. She had not heard it ring, so the call had to be his own. She deposited the tray on a low glass table and took a seat on the white wool chesterfield next to it, leaning back against the curve of the arm and trying consciously not to listen. In spite of herself, she found her eyes drawn to the figure seated opposite, meeting his steady regard with a sudden rush of warmth under her skin. She hoped it didn't show. Her actions so far hardly suggested a blushing violet.

'Tuesday, then,' he said into the receiver. 'Seven-thirty in the American Bar.'

Gemma tore her gaze away as he replaced the instrument in its rest. Nothing he had said confirmed the sex of the person to whom he had been speaking, yet an evening appointment suggested a woman. Was he capable, she wondered, of leaving her here alone while he met another woman? She wouldn't put it past him.

'It's going to be tight,' he commented, reaching for his cup. 'I wasn't counting on taking a holiday.'

'A working holiday, surely?' Gemma corrected lightly.

'With compensations,' he agreed, eyes glinting at the swift run of expression across her face. 'We're going to have to get you properly kitted out—at least, you'll have it to do. You'd better go see Sally Rogers again.'

Gemma's chin came up a fraction. 'Don't you trust me to choose a suitable wardrobe on my own?'

'Frankly, no. Not if your original outfit was an example.' He was quite unapologetic about it. 'When I'm doing the paying, I expect to lay down the rules.'

'You mean no fiancée of yours—real or otherwise—is going to make you ashamed of her?'

'Something like that.' The sarcasm failed to stir him. 'I have a certain reputation to think about.'

'That I don't doubt!'

'Hey.' His tone was soft, but with an underlying note not to be ignored. 'Our arrangement carries no ties—on either side. If you don't like it, you're at liberty to walk right out of here any time you want to.'

It was pride alone that brought her to her feet, body rigid. 'You don't need to say that twice. I'll get my things right now!'

He caught her before she reached the staircase, swinging her round and into his arms without heeding her protest. Locked against that strong, hard body, Gemma felt herself melting—felt the anger and mortification fade under the calculated assault on her senses. He had her right where he wanted her, and he knew it; it was there in his eyes when he lifted his head to look at her.

'You're not going anywhere,' he said. 'Unless it's to bed.' He was smiling again, the wicked glint an invitation in itself. 'Did you ever make love in the afternoon?'

'Logan——' she was trembling, torn between different needs, 'I don't think——'

'Then don't,' he advised. 'Just feel. That's what it's all about.'

He lifted her without effort and carried her up the open flight, placing her in the centre of the huge, fluffy duvet covering the bed. She watched his hand go up to loosen his tie; brown and fleshless; so sure in its every movement. A core of heat was gathering deep inside her, rising to overwhelm every last vestige of reluctance. She felt weightless, yet was aware of every tiny nerve ending as if her skin had been peeled back to leave them raw. To move was beyond her. She just lay there waiting for him to come to her.

He stripped completely before doing so, unselfconscious in his nudity as he knelt over her. Her own clothing was deftly removed and discarded, her body exposed to his gaze in the full light of day from the uncurtained window.

He took his time in studying it, lingering on the firm swell of her breasts, the curve of waist and hip, sliding over the smooth tautness of her stomach to the shadowed joining of her thighs.

'Quality,' he murmured. 'In every aspect, you have quality, Gemma. I want this to last!'

He meant only now, she told herself as he put his lips to her throat, not for ever. To a man like Logan there was no forever. He lived for the moment. If she wanted to hold him even for a little while she had to learn to do the same. Forget about next year, next week—even tomorrow. Right here and now was all that mattered.

There were times during the days following when Gemma was to revise that statement; times when she wished she had never set eyes on Logan Telford. Apart from the nights themselves, she saw little of him. There was always some business commitment—at least, he said it was business; she had no way of being sure. In his kind of work there was no such thing as regular hours, he told her on the one occasion when she did bring up the subject. He had fingers in other pies apart from the one in which she was involved. Gemma could believe that. It was about the only aspect of him in which she could place any trust.

By Thursday afternoon she had completed her own preparations for the coming trip, apart from packing the smaller items of toilet ware. Logan was out when she arrived back at the studio around three after lunch with Sally Rogers. Not that she had really anticipated any different.

Over the past four days she and Sally had become quite friendly. It was only from the latter that she had learned anything about Logan's background, and at that the information was sketchy. Born in England, he had spent a large part of his teen years in the States, only returning to his own country on the death of his father. His mother was still alive, but her present whereabouts was unknown. Sally had said he rarely spoke of her. Their own relationship went back some five or six years—another burned-out affair, to quote Sally herself. She seemed to bear no grudge. Gemma hoped she would be capable of the same degree of acceptance if and when her own turn came.

The 'if' had crept in despite all her efforts to convince herself of the impermanency of their arrangement. They were so good together—when they were together. It didn't seem possible that something so right could go wrong. Logan had said it himself only the previous night: a rare communion, he had called it. And not only in lovemaking either. They were attuned in so many ways.

Watching the river traffic from the patio, Gemma allowed herself the luxury of imagining a future for the two of them. She could even share in his work. Not living here, though. This was no home in which to bring up a family.

Smiling wryly to herself, she brought her thoughts to a halt at that point. Even allowing for everything else, Logan was no family man.

By eight o'clock it had become obvious that he was not coming home for a meal. Gemma grilled a lone steak and pushed it resolutely down an unwilling throat, along with a little salad. There was no point in going without food simply because some man was making her miserable. One had to eat to stay healthy.

Except that Logan was not just some man, she acknowledged bitterly in the end. He was everything to her. Trust her to choose someone who could never be relied upon to return her feelings. Why hadn't she turned tail and run that very first day! Whoever had said, ''tis better to have loved and lost than never to have loved at all,' hadn't known what they were talking about.

By ten-thirty the self-pity had turned to something approaching fury, the latter emotion aided not a little by the bottle of wine she had opened. What right, she asked herself, did he have to invite her into his home and then leave her alone this way? She was his guest. She deserved consideration. When he did put in an appearance she was going to tell him so, and in no uncertain terms!

She spent the next hour or so deliberating exactly what she was going to say, rejecting one choice phrase in favour of another until her mind finally gave up on the whole idea when the clock showed midnight. Perhaps he wasn't going to return at all that night, she thought, sinking back into her former despondency. She had no idea where he might be—or with whom. The best thing she could do was go to bed. There was nothing to stay up for. Not any more.

The wine she had drunk was making her head feel light, almost as if it were detached from her body. Struggling out of her clothing, she left the garments lying where they had fallen and collapsed on to the bed, giggling as a tiny escaped feather tickled her nose. Swansdown, she told herself tipsily. She was floating on swansdown! Drifting far, far away——

The light run of a fingertip the length of her spine dragged her back from the depths of a sleep seemingly only just begun. She tried to burrow deeper into the softness of the quilt, murmuring a peevish little protest.

'You should have left some in the bottle,' said Logan on a note of amusement. Ruthlessly he turned her over, mouth widening sardonically at the involuntary movement of her arm to shield her eyes from the light. 'I know the perfect cure for a hangover.'

Gemma made no move as he bent his head to find her lips. He had taken off his jacket but was still wearing his shirt; she could feel the smooth coolness of the material against her skin, the hardness of the buttons. There was familiarity in the movement of the hand circling her breast, a suggestion of ownership. She stiffened to the touch, pushing him roughly away.

'Don't imagine you can just walk in here any time you like, and do as you like!' she spat at him with a vehemence that surprised even herself. 'I'm not a commodity for your exclusive use!'

He didn't let her go, simply sat there looking at her with faintly lifted brows. 'While you're here with me you'd better be,' he said. 'What you do afterwards, of course, is entirely your own affair.'

It was the latter statement that hurt the most, revealing as it did the total lack of depth in his regard for her. Aware of the fact she might have been; having it put into words was something else again. Her reaction was instinctive, one hand coming up with fingers curved to rake the lean, dark face, only it never connected because his reactions were even swifter, his grasp on her wrist drawing a faint hiss of pain through her teeth.

'Don't try it,' he warned with silky softness. 'I don't have any gallant notions about turning the other cheek. If we're going to fight we do it on equal terms. That means no nails for a start.'

'You're hurting me!' she whispered, trying to prise his fingers open from about her wrist. 'Logan!——'

'You started it,' he responded on the same soft note. 'We'll take it from there.'

Anger flooded through her, lending her a strength she had not known she possessed. Her sudden movement took him by surprise too, his fingers relaxing their grip as she jerked herself away from him. Next moment she was on her feet and running for the one place where she could slide a bolt and shut him out. Spending the rest of the night in the bathroom was not exactly conducive with creature comfort, but anything was preferable to the alternative. Logan would never have her again. She would make sure of it. Come the morning she was leaving for good. Let him stew!

She hadn't believed him capable of the speed with which he followed her. Before she could even close the door again, much less slide the bolt, he was on her, eyes gleaming with an unholy light as he shoved her back against the cold tiled wall. His mouth was like a vice, pinning hers beneath it with a pressure she couldn't withstand. Only when her lips parted did he temper the demand, exploring the sensitive inner flesh with slow sensuality until she began to respond in spite of herself.

The carpeted floor felt warm to her back after the chill of the tiles. Kneeling astride her, Logan stripped off his shirt and tossed it into the bath, coming down to her again to flick his tongue from her navel to the valley between her breasts in one taunting sweep. She writhed under him as he closed his lips over one pink, inviting nipple, feeling the subtle bite of his teeth; whimpering with the pleasure that was so close to pain. There was no room left in her mind for anything beyond this moment. She wanted only what he wanted—all that he wanted. At which point he removed the rest of his clothing she could never be sure. All she remembered was the heat of flesh against flesh, the sliding together and the thunder of her own heartbeats in her ears as climax came simultaneously for them both.

Later, after Logan had carried her back to bed, there was time for rational thought again. Lying there in the hard circle of his arms, Gemma stared into the darkness and wondered how she could ever have imagined she might just walk away from all this. Loving Logan was not only foolish, it was downright futile, yet love him she did. Why, she wasn't at all sure. He was by no means the kindest of men: he could even be said to be devoid of the gentler emotions altogether. Only knowing that made little difference.

'Go to sleep,' he murmured suddenly, surprising her because she had thought him already in that welcome state. 'I can feel your mind revolving from here!'

He probably knew just what it was revolving

around too, she acknowledged with irony. Not that it would worry him a great deal. He hadn't asked her to fall in love with him. If anything he had done everything to put her off the very idea. It was her own cross to bear.

The airport was thronged, their flight delayed by thirty minutes. In the past, Gemma had found flying boring. With Logan at her side, time itself flew on oiled wheels. By degrees she led him round to talk about the theatre, expressing as much interest in and knowledge of the profession as she dared without giving herself away.

'You've a quick grasp,' he admitted on a note of approbation at one point. 'My present secretary is leaving me in a week or two. Maybe we could come to some arrangement whereby she shows you the ropes before she goes. It would solve your job problems, and save a load of interviews.'

He was beginning to believe in the fictional background they had concocted for her, Gemma realised wryly. Her typing was strictly of the two-fingered variety. She let that particular aspect lie, slanting a glance at the hard-angled profile. 'We may not be together in a few weeks' time.'

His shrug made light of the statement. 'Not in the same sense, perhaps. What difference need that make?'

'Quite a lot, I should imagine.'

'Meaning that two people who've shared a bed can't maintain a friendly relationship away from it?' He was looking her way now, smile twisted. 'That hasn't been my experience up to now.'

If Sally Rogers was any example, Gemma

could almost believe it. The former's whole attitude towards Logan suggested a total lack of animosity. When she spoke of him it was with fond reminiscence. She was not, however, his only past affair.

'Including Caryn?' she asked blandly.

Grey eyes held a familiar spark. 'You've a bad habit of shoving her in my face. I told you before, Caryn is a different proposition.'

'That isn't what you just said.'

'Are you trying to get my goat?' he demanded. 'I need a secretary, not a mentor! Could be it wasn't such a great idea.'

It had been a lousy idea, Gemma reflected, although with the right qualifications she might have been tempted to take him up on it. What price pride?

Last night still remained vivid in her mind's eye, the memory alone enough to curl her stomach muscles. For the first time it occurred to her to wonder about the accommodation aboard the yacht. As an ostensibly engaged couple, it was possible that they might be offered a cabin together, although if Caryn had anything to do with the allocation that possibility was remote. Separation at this point would be more than she could bear. Even if Logan was prepared to journey between cabins at night, it wouldn't be the same.

'How big is this yacht?' she heard herself asking, and felt his glance.

'Big enough to take eight passengers plus three crew. Work it out for yourself.'

'Eight? I thought it was just going to be the four of us?'

'Just one other couple, Rob said. Nobody I know. Does it matter?'

Gemma didn't suppose it did. Not now the act had come so much closer to reality. Closer? She had to smile a little. There was no act on her part. Not any longer. The character had taken over all the way down the line!

They took a taxi directly from the Athens' airport to the vast dock area of Piraeus. The afternoon heat was enervating. Gemma welcomed the opened windows and the wind in her face, confident in the knowledge that her hair would fall back into place with just a shake of her head. To travel in, she had worn a lightweight trouser suit in pale cream. With the jacket removed to reveal the thin black tunic top, she felt ready for any event.

The yacht itself was moored offshore in one of the semi-circular basins facing south towards Aegina, long and white and luxurious. A boat was waiting to take them out from the crescent-shaped waterfront with its bordering of open-air cafés, captained by a young Greek whose dark-eyed appraisal of Gemma was in no way moderated by Logan's presence. His name was Spiros, he told them in passably good English. Should they have any desires, he would be only too happy to fulfil them.

The latter offer was made with the dark eyes boldly on Gemma's face, his inference un-ashamedly obvious. She half anticipated some cutting reply from Logan, but he appeared not to have noticed, gazing towards the yacht as if in search of something—or someone.

It was Robert who met them at the head of the

gangway. Clad in white shorts and tee-shirt, with
his legs already browned, he looked very much
the same person Gemma had last seen the
previous Sunday morning at the poolside. That
he was genuinely pleased to see the two of them
was evidenced by a smile which reached right
into his eyes.

'Caryn went to lie down,' he said. 'Too much
sun, I think. I'll take you straight down to your
cabins, then you can get into something more
comfortable. Swimsuits and shorts are the order
of the day.'

Cabins, he had said. Gemma's spirits took a
nosedive. Caryn's hand again. It had to be.
Robert would never have thought of parting
them.

There was no particular reaction from Logan.
He seemed to accept the situation as normal. To a
man there was probably little problem. Either he
came to her cabin or she went to his. Simple. If it
had to be it had to be, Gemma conceded wryly,
only there was no way she was going to be the
one doing the flitting around!

As might have been anticipated, the cabins
themselves were well fitted out. The single to
which she was shown contained a second berth
which let down out of the wall above the bed,
converting it to the occasional double. Gemma
herself would have happily settled for that
arrangement right now. Just to share the same
space with Logan would be enough.

He wasn't even on the same length of corridor,
although because of the design of the boat they
actually shared a bulkhead.

'I'll have to teach you Morse code,' he said on

a lightly mocking note, coming to stand in her doorway after Robert had left them. 'Three dots, three dashes, three dots, and I'll be round in a flash. Not that it will be your soul I'll be after saving!'

'I don't know how you can joke about it,' she said flatly. 'You know Caryn arranged it this way!'

'Very likely. On the other hand, it's quite possible there are only a couple of double staterooms, and they're already taken.' His shrug made light of the statement. 'No big deal. We're not light years away from each other.'

'Providing you don't expect me to do any travelling!'

The retort came out sharper than she had intended, lifting dark brows in sudden, specula-tive assessment. 'Just be here when I want you,' he said. 'That's all I ask.'

Gemma bit her lip, aware that she had asked for that. She bent her head to her open suitcase, jumping when Logan put a hand on her arm because she hadn't heard him move.

'Don't go heavy on me,' he said softly. 'A clinging woman I can do without.' He turned her towards him, putting a finger under her chin to study her uptilted face, the veiled green eyes. The smile came unwillingly, almost as if he resented her ability to draw it from him. '"Nor custom stale her infinite variety",' he quoted on a dry note. 'So far you've kept me off balance all the way!'

And the moment she stopped doing that she lost her appeal, she gathered. It was on the tip of her tongue to tell him there and then that the affair was over, but she lacked the guts to go that far. Chauvinist or not, he was the man she wanted—even needed.

'I'm just a bit tired after the journey,' she said, summoning a smile of her own. 'A shower and a change of clothes, and I'll be on top again.'

The quirk of the mobile left eyebrow weakened her at the knees. 'Sounds interesting. Why don't we pass up the shower and go straight to bed?'

'Robert said there'd be tea waiting,' she reminded him, fighting the sensations rising in her at the touch of the lean fingers on her nape.

'At five,' he responded. 'It's only just gone four. We have all the time in the world.'

Gemma didn't have it in her to make any further demur. They helped each other undress, savouring the delicious coolness of the air-conditioning. It was Logan who sank first on to the bed, pulling her down to him with the familiar spark lighting his eyes. 'Be gentle with me,' he said.

Laughing, loving him, she put her head down to his chest and used the tip of her tongue to score a swift and delicate line from his breast bone down through the wiry tangle of hair on his chest to the pit of his navel, reversing the technique he had used on her the night before. Every muscle in his body tensed in anticipation, his breathing increasing in depth and rate as she traced each pulsing nerve path, sought out every sensitive crevice. For the first time she had him at her mercy, his whole being concentrated on the flickering fire scorching his flesh; his features drawn into the same agonised grimace her own knew so well.

'Don't stop,' he groaned. 'For God's sake don't stop!'

Gemma was beyond stopping anything, her senses roused to flash point. With Logan she was another person, a complete woman. She wanted to give him the same overwhelming, mind-blasting pleasure he had given her so many times this past week. Loving him was only a part of it. He was an extension of her: essential to life. If there was any way at all that she could make him feel that same need of her then she would find it. One way or another she would find it!

CHAPTER SIX

THE spacious afterdeck was partially shaded by a
white awning under which was set a circular table
and several chairs. There were loungers beyond,
grouped around a small oval swimming pool.
Emerging from the body of the ship with Logan
at her back, Gemma could see only one of the
latter occupied, the rest of the group obviously
preferring a more upright and cooler seat.

They were apparently the last of the party
out. From the twinkle in Robert's eye as he
stood up to greet them, he had a very good idea
why.

'Come and meet the rest of the gang,' he
invited. 'Clem and Beryl Arkwright—Gemma
Holt; Logan Telford.'

The other couple were in their mid-forties, the
woman auburn-rinsed and unashamedly over-
weight in her two-piece suit, her husband as lean
as a rail, with a thatch of sandy hair lifted by the
faint breeze coming off the water. They seemed a
pleasant, unassuming pair. Gemma could imagine
Robert might find them restful.

What Caryn thought of them was anyone's
guess. Her chair was placed a few feet away from
the other three, as if she wished to isolate herself
from general conversation. Her figure was shown
to some advantage by the black bikini, the cut of
the bra top extreme. In her own bright yellow
suit, Gemma felt almost overdressed by com-

parison—and wholly immature.

Caryn ignored her, the blue eyes seeking only those of the man accompanying her.

'Good flight?' she asked.

'As flights go,' he responded, taking a seat at Gemma's side. 'We took off and we landed—the bit in between doesn't vary much.'

'But a charming travelling companion makes a difference, surely,' put in Clem with somewhat heavy-handed gallantry, and drew a slow smile.

'Oh, sure!'

'Logan thinks women are for looking at, not listening to,' said Gemma lightly. She wrinkled her nose at him, secure in the memory of the past hour, seeing his eyes darken, his mouth take on a faint but meaningful slant. Never could two people have been closer than they had been; have achieved such total completeness. She wanted him again, right now. It was an ache deep inside her.

Caryn was watching them, her expression icily controlled. Gemma no longer cared. Whatever the other woman had been to Logan once, it was over.

'Incidentally,' said Robert on a casual note, 'I should mention our unexpected addition to the party. Sleeping Beauty over there turned up out of the blue on Monday. What else could we do but have him tag along!'

Logan had switched his gaze to the other man's face, eyes suddenly narrowed. Robert met the look with bland assurance. 'It appears he finally got tired of theatre in the rough. He's home for a spell until he finds something else he wants to do.'

'Wanting is one thing—'Logan's tone was dry'—opportunity another.'

The smile took little account of implied rejection. 'But contacts are always useful.'

Gemma scarcely heard the exchange. She felt frozen into her chair. From here, all she could see of the subject under discussion was the top of a fair head. If he was awake he was giving no sign. Her mind refused to function on any useful level. Eventually she and Jason Powell were going to come face to face. What she was going to say to him she had no idea. The only thing clear to her was that somehow she had to keep Logan from learning the truth this way.

'It's so hot,' she heard her own voice saying. 'I think I'll take a dip in the pool.' She was on her feet without conscious effort, her movements astonishingly calm and unhurried.

'I'll have a Daiquiri waiting for you when you come out,' promised Robert, and she lifted a hand in acknowledgement.

'I'll look forward to it!'

The water refreshed her mind as well as her body. Surfacing, she stretched out her limbs and let herself float, moving her hands very gently to steer herself in the right direction. Only when she was certain that none of the others were taking any interest in her actions did she come slowly upright, grasping the pool rim at the point closest to where Jason lounged. He was wearing a pair of scarlet racing trunks which left little to the imagination, his slim, supple body already turning a golden bronze in the sun. The features beneath the over-long thicket of curly hair were almost too perfectly formed, bordering on a beauty that could have come close to feminine had it not been for the beard covering his lower jawline. He bore no resemblance whatsoever to his father.

Her voice was a mere whisper of sound. 'Jason!'

The deceptively lazy brown eyes came open with reluctance, his head moving in unison to discover the source of interruption. Recognition was far from instant, the smile he summoned taking whole seconds to lose its calculated appeal and stiffen into disbelief.

'Gemma?' he said with disturbing clarity. 'What the hell?——'

'Be quiet—please!' she muttered, trying to infuse urgency without raising her voice. 'Jason, you have to do me a favour. I'm relying on you!'

He studied her for a long moment, expression mingling uncertainty and curiosity in roughly equal amounts. 'Don't tell me you're the fiancée Telford was bringing with him?' he said at last. 'When did that happen?'

It was an awkward question. She sidestepped as best she could. 'We'll talk about that later. I want you to pretend we've never met.'

'Why?' Curiosity had taken precedence now, the brown eyes bright with it.

'It would take too long to explain.' She cast a hasty glance over her shoulder at the group beneath the awning, relieved that no one appeared to be taking any particular note of their conversation. Nevertheless, she was going to have to be quick. Everything depended on Jason's reaction. 'We've never met, and I don't have anything to do with theatre,' she added, treading water to keep herself upright as her fingers began to tire of gripping the hard rim. 'I'll tell you everything the first chance I get. Just go along with me for now!'

'For old times' sake?' His mouth tilted. 'Okay, you got yourself a deal. It has to be pretty important to make you this uptight.'

'It is.' She said it with emphasis. 'It really is!'

'I see you two have introduced yourselves.' Robert was standing on the poolside opposite, his approach unobserved by either of them. His glance encompassed both faces, taking on a certain speculation in the process. 'I keep forgetting how casually you young folk deal with the social niceties. Are you ready to rejoin the party?'

'As ready as we'll ever be,' said Jason flippantly. He stood up, taking the towel from the lounger behind him and holding it out with a devilish little grin. 'Come on over to the ladder and I'll give you a rub down.'

'There are plenty of clean towels,' put in his father. 'And I'm quite sure Gemma is more than capable of using one on herself.'

'Not as much fun, though.' Still grinning, Jason dropped the towel back on the lounger and extended a hand instead. 'I'll save you the trouble of swimming across.'

The ladder he had spoken of was only bare feet away, but to refuse the offer would, Gemma thought, place too much importance on the moment. She laughed and took the hand, propelling herself upwards as he pulled. Jason made no attempt to move back, seizing her under the elbows to steady her balance, his body so close she could feel the sun-stoked heat emanating from him. 'You've altered your hairstyle,' he observed, still holding her. 'I liked the old Gemma!'

The old Gemma doesn't exist any more, she wanted to say, only now was hardly the time. All eyes were on them; all conversation suddenly ceased. She detached herself from the unresisting hands and walked on past him, the smile pasted into place. Jason waited a bare moment before following her.

Towelling the excess moisture from her hair and limbs gave her time to calm her nerves. When the moment came to meet Logan's level gaze she was able to do so with an outward insouciance. Had she been honest with him from the start none of this need have mattered, but it was too late to go back. She could only place her trust in Jason's word.

A woman in her late thirties wearing white shorts and cotton tee-shirt came to replenish their drinks. Robert introduced her to the latecomers as Ida Rourke who would be doing all the catering on board. Her husband was Captain. Come the end of the season in late October, Robert added after she had left, they would run the boat down to Rhodes for the winter, disturbed only when the owners themselves chose to fly out for a long weekend. To Gemma it sounded an idyllic existence.

The whole party stayed on deck drinking and chatting until after darkness fell. Dinner was to be served on board at eight-thirty. It was Robert who laughingly suggested they should all of them make a move.

'Dress informal,' he stipulated. 'Ties don't go with the climate.'

'May be as well, seeing I didn't bring one,' drawled his son, tossing off the last of his drink. His eyes sought Gemma's as he got to his feet. 'My cabin is next door to yours. If you need any help just knock!'

There was a small silence as he sauntered away. Robert looked faintly embarrassed. 'His idea of a joke,' he said lamely to Logan. 'Ignore it.'

The answering shrug was light. 'I intend to.'

The rest of the party dispersed to their cabins *en masse*. Shutting her own door, Gemma wondered if Logan's lack of personal communication with her this past hour had been deliberate or not. Certainly his change of attitude stemmed from that moment by the pool when Jason had pulled her out.

Jealousy was a destroying emotion, she knew, yet Logan was hardly the type to give way. Perhaps she had been wrong in assuming that her sly approach to speak to Jason had not been noted. If he had seen her, Logan would no doubt consider any subsequent familiarity entirely her fault, which would explain the way he had looked at her on her return. Not jealousy so much as possessiveness. What was his was his alone until such time as he decided otherwise. There had been a time when Gemma would have found that whole notion ridiculous in concept, only not any more, because she felt exactly the same: except that for her the feeling was permanent.

She had showered and was making up her eyes at the dressing mirror when the light tap came on the door. Pulling the belt of her towelling robe a little tighter about her waist, she went to open it, stepping back in disconcertion as Jason moved quickly into the cabin.

'So what's it all about?' he asked, standing with hands thrust into the pockets of his cotton drill slacks and a look of determination on his face. 'If I'm going to play the role I need to be motivated.'

'It's a long story,' she said a little desperately.

'So condense it.'

She did so as best as she was able, drawing no response from him until she had finished, and then only a slow, ironic shaking of the head.

'You've certainly landed yourself in it! From what I know of Telford, he isn't the type to forgive and forget being made a fool of.'

'I never tried to make a fool of him,' Gemma denied. 'One thing led to another, that's all.'

'And now you're in love with the guy and you don't know how to handle the situation.'

'Yes.' She paused, biting her lip. 'Do I make it so obvious?'

'The way you feel about him?' Jason shrugged again. 'Probably not to anybody who doesn't know you. You never agonised over my opinion of you the same way, that's for sure!' He smiled at the fleeting change of expression in her eyes. 'No complaints. We never did get too involved. You realise he's going to have to know the truth some time, of course? Unless you intend giving up the theatre altogether, that is.'

Gemma gazed at him unhappily. 'You're saying I should tell him before he finds out some other way?'

'Seems common sense to me. Reading between the lines, I'd say the sooner the better.'

'But isn't he going to think I only slept with him because I wanted a part in the show?'

'Naturally. You'll just have to convince him that his superb technique drove all ambition of that nature right out of your head.' Jason appeared to be enjoying himself. 'You're an able enough actress, Gemma—at least, you were. It shouldn't be too difficult a part to tackle.'

'Thanks.' Her tone was dry. 'You're a tremendous help!'

'What would you expect? The only one who can get you out of trouble is yourself. The best I can do for you is steer clear.'

'The way you did at the pool?'

'Ah, now that was purely involuntary. When you pull Aphrodite from the waves the first impulse is to kiss her hallo!'

Gemma had to laugh. In this mood, with face so hotly shining innocent, Jason could cut through anger like a knife through butter. 'You're impossible,' she said. 'You always were!'

'But you loved me, just a little bit?' His tone was suddenly softer. 'How about that kiss—for old times' sake?'

'I don't think so.' Green eyes took on a faint glint. 'You're too capable of making me forget my priorities.'

His grin was derisive. 'Try not to be too obvious. Telford isn't just out of the egg! Good luck, anyway.'

She was going to need it, Gemma thought ruefully as the door closed again behind him. Acting skill alone would hardly be enough.

Dinner was served on the afterdeck under the awning, with canvas covers laced over the deck rails in order to cut the breeze to a minimum. Aromatic candles placed at intervals about the deck served to keep insects at bay.

Gemma found herself seated between Clem and Jason at the round table, an arrangement which left Caryn dividing her attention between her stepson and Logan, with predictable results. Robert appeared to have noticed nothing unusual in the placings, but Gemma already knew him too well to take that indifference at face value. Far from convincing his wife of the futility of seeking to rekindle old flames, he seemed to have provided her with fuel to stoke the fire. If only for Robert's sake, Gemma reflected, she should take steps to ensure Logan's unavailability.

She started that very campaign as soon as the meal was over, and the table moved back to allow room for those who wanted to dance to the music taped up from the salon stereo system, drifting across to Logan's side of the deck on the ostensible excuse of looking at the shore lights from a closer vantage point. When she turned again he was only a couple of feet away, his back to her as he listened to whatever it was Caryn was whispering with such apparent urgency. Taking a deep breath, Gemma moved forward and slid her hand through his arm, smiling up into the eyes looking round at her.

'Dance, darling?'

The pause was brief, the slant of his mouth too familiar. 'One of these days I'll teach you to wait till you're asked,' he said lightly. 'Excuse us, Caryn.'

Gemma caught the other's angry glare before she turned away, and stemmed a surge of purely feminine satisfaction. The victor could afford to be generous. Sliding into Logan's arms as they took to the floor, she resisted the need to press herself against him and looked up into the grey eyes, trying to assess his mood without particular success.

'Are you angry with me over something?' she asked, taking the line of direct attack.

His expression didn't alter. 'Such as what?'

She laughed. 'I always thought that was supposed to be a feminine trait!'

'Which just goes to show one should never generalise.' He studied the face raised to him, lifting an eyebrow faintly. 'You feel tense. Guilty conscience?'

Gemma would not have been human had she been able to control all reaction. The attack was not to be one-sided. She forced herself to hold his gaze, even now searching her mind for an easy way out. Only there was none. The only thing she could play for was a little more time to collect her thoughts.

'If you mean there's something I haven't told you, then I suppose you're right,' she admitted. 'It's been a case of finding the right moment.'

'Anything wrong with now?'

'Well, yes. It's going to take time.'

He was still revealing little. 'Maybe you should start with Jason.'

This time her responses were wholly obvious. Heart thudding painfully, she slid her eyes away from his. 'How did you guess?'

His laugh held irony. 'There had to be some good reason for that fast approach you made this afternoon. While I'm willing to acknowledge he's a fascinating character, I doubt if he can pull the birds through the back of his head!'

'You don't have to jeer,' she said, forcing herself to look at him directly again. 'Jason might not be your idea of the macho male, but he doesn't need to be.'

'Meaning he has other attributes?'

Green eyes flashed. 'At least he knows how to listen!'

'When there's anything worth listening to.' His hold had tightened at her back. 'One point you should get clear. I might be curious as to how you came to know him at all, but that's as far as it goes. We're here and now. No past.'

And precious little future, Gemma thought numbly. All right, so if that was the way he wanted it, that was the way she would play it. 'In that case, there's no point in going into it,' she said.

'None at all, providing you keep him at arm's length from here on in.'

Gemma searched the strong, chiselled features, looking deep into steady grey eyes. 'Are you always so totally possessive?' she asked at length.

'I don't like sharing,' Logan admitted. 'Neither do you.'

She was bound to acknowledge the truth in that statement. The very thought of Logan with another woman—any other woman—was anathema to her. She smiled suddenly, casting aside all other concerns as she slid her hands up and over his shoulders to bring herself closer against him. This was what mattered—the two of them together. Let the future take care of itself.

She danced with Clem after that, and then with

Jason, telling herself Logan could hardly expect her to take that arm's length instruction too literally when he himself was holding Caryn a great deal closer than that at present.

'Got it over with yet?' Jason asked in a stage whisper, and she trod deliberately on his foot, making him wince.

'You're not funny!' she hissed.

'Sorry. My mistake.' This time he kept it down to a conspiratorial murmur. 'Did you tell him?'

'He knows we're not strangers.' Gemma kept her tone to a normal low conversational pitch. 'The rest he's not interested in.'

'Did he get the chance to decide?'

'I just told you, he didn't want to hear. So far as Logan is concerned, the past is a closed book.'

'That's the worst line I ever heard you use.' The jeer was calculated to needle her. 'I take it you've given up any idea you ever had of getting a part in the show? Is any man worth it?'

'I think so.' She refused to allow the reminder of what she *was* giving up to sink in too deeply. 'There'll be other parts.'

'And a lot of people after them. We have to use any advantage we can get—you know that. You're a fool if you let anything come before your career.'

'So I'm a fool.' She waited a moment before adding softly, 'You're only here yourself because you heard Logan was going to be in the party, aren't you? Who told you?'

'Dad did. He phoned me at our last stop in Crewe and suggested I join the party, though lord only knows how he found out which town we were playing. We weren't even sure of our own itinerary more than a couple of days or so in advance.'

'Which part are you after?'

'The male dancing lead—what else? I'm no great shakes as a singer, even if I had the physique to start throwing my weight about the stage! Anyway, Trevor Sullivan has already accepted. With him and Berrisford to draw the crowds, I'd say the show can't fail.' He drew back a little to look at her questioningly. 'Something wrong?'

Gemma forced herself to relax, smiling and shaking her head. 'Goose walked over my grave. You do mean Adele Berrisford, I suppose?'

'Is there any other? She's only just finished a Broadway run, so they're lucky to get her. Not that I'm sure it's actually finalised yet. That could be one of the reasons Dad's playing cagey over the backing. He didn't go into too much detail.'

He paused, adjusting his movements to keep the two of them in the same bare corner of the deck, hands lightly at her waist. 'You know, you'd make a great Bianca. In fact we'd make a great pair! Remember that number we put together for the end-of-year show?' Still holding on to her, he executed a couple of steps from it, laughing at the expression on her face. 'A little adjustment and we could even perform to this piece they're playing right now. Might be all that's needed.'

'No!' Her voice came out sharper and louder than she had intended, increasing attention already drawn their way by Jason's exhibition. She toned it down, not daring to look round.

'Stop playing the fool, will you! It's my life you'll be messing up!'

'Only a minor part of it,' he responded hardily. 'How long do you think you and Telford are going to last? Dad's known him for years. His women are legend! Caryn was only one of them. You're not starting to believe in this engagement of yours, by any chance? I thought that was purely for Dad's benefit.'

'It is.' Gemma could feel her jaw aching from the tautness of muscle, but she still refused to give way. 'So I need my head examining. What difference does it make to you? You can angle for your own audition.'

'Oh, I'll get it, never fear. Dad doesn't mess around when it comes to making a deal.'

'You mean you come with the backing?'

'The audition does. What I make of it is my lookout.'

'You'd have to shave off the beard,' she warned him.

'Then I'll shave off the beard. I can always grow it again later.' The pause held deliberation. 'There's little I wouldn't do to get ahead. Not with all those others out there fighting for the same cause. I once thought we shared the same kind of ambition.'

'We did—we do.' Gemma stopped unhappily. 'You were never in love, Jason.'

'Not to the point of losing my reason. I hope you can look back later and think it was worth it.'

Gemma hoped so too. If she had thought the future insecure before it was doubly so now. With her mother involved there was little chance of escaping eventual discovery. The only safe way out was to make a full confession here and now.

On the other hand, rehearsals wouldn't be starting for weeks, by which time her affair with Logan could well be over anyway. Could she risk losing what she had for the sake of what might happen? She had to think about it before she acted.

Murmuring something about changing for a swim, Jason left her close by where his father was sitting alone looking at the sea, and vanished below. Gemma slid into a seat alongside her host and leaned an arm on the rail the way he was doing, gazing into the starlit water.

'I haven't seen you dancing,' she said.

'Probably because I don't enjoy dancing.' He was smiling, though not in any humorous fashion. 'One more nail in my coffin, would you say?'

She needed no explanation of what he was talking about. 'I don't see why,' she said. 'Caryn must have known that before she married you.'

'She knew a lot of things before she married me. That doesn't make it any easier to accept.' The smile was still there. 'Frankly, I bore her.'

'I'm sure that's not true!'

'Oh, I rather think it is. She only sleeps with me under protest.' He caught Gemma's movement and quickly put out a hand to stay her. 'All right, I shouldn't have said that. I've had too much to drink and I'm losing my grip. Don't run away.'

'I wasn't running,' she denied. 'I just thought you might prefer to be alone.'

'I'm too much alone.' The smile turned to a

grin, deliberate this time. 'And downright maudlin with it! That's the gin for you.'

'Then don't have any more,' she suggested, eyeing the glass in his hand.

Robert followed her glance, mouth twisting afresh. 'You're right, of course. It doesn't mix well with the tablets.'

'Tablets for what?' she asked on a note of concern. 'I didn't realise——'

'Sleeping,' he interrupted before she could finish. 'Just sleeping. Insomnia is a long-standing complaint. Too active a mind, I'm told.' He changed the subject abruptly. 'Enjoying the break so far?'

'Very much.' Gemma had already debated whether or not to mention her former association with Jason and decided against it. Robert was not going to accept that bare statement of fact; he was going to want some detail. Better to leave things the way they were. 'I've never been to Greece before,' she added. 'I'd like to take the opportunity of seeing the Parthenon before I leave—if there's going to be time.'

'We'll make time. Everyone should see it at least once—preferably by moonlight. Too late tonight, I think, but we could always delay the cruise another day. Either that, or catch it when we get back from the islands. The choice is yours.'

'When we get back,' she said, reluctant to be responsible for any alteration in plans. 'I'll look forward to it.'

Jason returned wearing the same brief trunks he had worn that afternoon. He passed them without pausing in his stride, diving straight into the pool with scarcely a splash. The water in his hair and beard glinted under the lights when he surfaced. He swam for the rim, turning to grin at those watching.

'It feels great! Why don't you all come on in?'

'Too crowded,' said his father. 'Anyway, I'm for bed.' His eyes sought his wife standing with Beryl and Logan a short distance away. 'Caryn?'

To the uninitiated the latter's answering smile and nod was all that a dutiful wife's should be. Only because she was looking for it did Gemma catch the flash of irritation in the fine blue eyes.

'I'll be right down,' she said.

Gemma caught Logan's eye, her silent question answered by the faint and fleeting wink. Leave it to me, she took it to mean. She fully intended to do so. Between now and the moment he came to her she had a difficult decision to make.

It was gone midnight already, and no hardship to break up the party. Gemma took her leave along with both Beryl and Caryn, waving a hand in adieu to Jason who was still in the pool. The other two men were finishing drinks over by the far rail. Gemma wondered if Logan would come straight to her cabin or call first at his own. She hoped the latter. It would give her a little more time.

There was a small clock let into the bulkhead by her bed. She sat watching the minute hand move inexorably round as she grappled with conflicting emotions. In the end the choice was made for her. To live each day with this on her mind would be more than she could bear. He would understand. She had to *make* him understand! Her happiness depended on it.

That same minute hand had moved all the way around the face before she finally came to the conclusion that he wasn't coming. Possibly she had mistaken the signal he had sent. It would be like him to choose this way of bringing her to heel. Resolute as she had been on the question of who did the visiting, her present state of mind would not allow her to leave matters in abeyance. She had to get it over with.

The boat was quiet as she made her way along the short length of alleyway connecting the cabin access areas, the only sounds the slapping of water against the hull and the faint hum of the generator. The soft closing of a door somewhere ahead brought her up short. Grateful for the dimness of the overhead lighting, she pressed herself against the nearest bulkhead as someone moved across the far end of the alley. Recognition was instant, her whole body tensing to the realisation that there was only one cabin Caryn could have come from.

CHAPTER SEVEN

WHOLE minutes passed before Gemma could bring herself to move. When she did it was not in the direction of her cabin but aft towards the deck gangway. She needed air to breathe: wholesome fresh air.

There was no one else in evidence, although a couple of the deck lights had been left on. Standing at the rail over by the pool, she looked out across the silvered sea and tried to sort out her thoughts.

First and foremost it was pretty apparent that Logan had never had any intention of coming to her cabin tonight. The arrangement with Caryn must have been made while they were dancing together. With Robert sedated by his own hand, there was little if any risk of being caught. But what about her? Surely Logan must have realised she would be waiting for him? Could he have been so certain she wouldn't come looking for him?

Right now she felt too miserable to be angry. That would come later. I don't like sharing, he had said, and she had believed it. She was still prepared to believe it. What he had not made clear was the strictly one-way basis of that statement.

So what now? she asked herself. If he thought so little of her that he could deceive her this way then was the relationship worth pursuing at all? She could gain some satisfaction by flinging her own duplicity in his face and letting him wonder who had been using whom, but she doubted she would do it when it came to the crunch. Love itself was surely worth little as an emotion if it could be undermined so easily.

The air was still and warm, the former breeze faded away. She was wearing nothing beneath the towelling robe. On impulse she slid out of it and dropped into the pool, striking out in a smooth sidestroke which brought her to the opposite rim in mere seconds.

She lost count of how many times she made that crossing, concentrating only on the movement, on the mind-blanking passage through the water, tiring herself physically because it was the only anodyne she knew. When she did finally come to a halt she had to cling to the rim in order to steady her breathing before making any attempt to climb out of the pool.

'Had enough?' asked Logan from the far side. 'Or were you thinking of trying for the Guinness Books of records?'

Gemma turned her head slowly, allowing her body to swing at the same time so that she was facing him, her arms stretched along the curve of the overflow. He was sitting on the same lounger Jason had occupied earlier, legs and feet bare beneath the short silk dressing gown. How long he might have been there she had no idea. From what he had just said, it had to be quite a time.

'I needed the exercise,' she said.

'So it appears.' There was a pause while he studied her, his expression hard to define with any accuracy. When he got to his feet it was with sudden purpose. 'I think I'll join you.'

She watched him shed the robe and dive into the pool, ducking her head against the splash of water. He had reached her before she could move, his hands seeking her hips as he surfaced, pulling her to him.

'I can stand here,' he said softly. 'Just! Let go. I'll hold you.'

Gemma gazed at him for a long suspended moment, seeing the slicked-back dark hair, the narrowed eyes, the drops of water running down the lean face to outline the shape of his upper lip; feeling the hardness of him against her, the growing tumult of her own desire.

'Bastard!' she hissed through clenched teeth, and brought up her knee.

The water robbed the gesture of much of its force, but it still reckoned, judging from the sharp intake of breath. The hands gripping her hips tightened into twin vices, his mouth taking on a frighteningly ruthless line. Pinioned against the pool side, Gemma was helpless to do anything but take whatever he had in mind.

His anger lasted bare moments: she could feel the effort it took to bring himself under control.

'Why?' he demanded.

'You know why, damn you!' Her mouth was trembling, as much from fury as fear. 'I saw her leaving your cabin. I saw her!'

'So you saw her.' He was still holding her hard enough to hurt, his fingers digging into her flesh. 'And what does that prove?'

She had anticipated an outright denial, not this counter-attack. It took the wind out of her, turning anger to uncertainty. Limbs rigid, she searched his eyes, trying to pierce the grey depths.

'It proves she was there,' she got out at last. 'Knowing you, I doubt if you were playing tiddley-winks!'

'You don't know me,' he said. 'We've shared a bed, nothing more.' He was speaking in low, clipped tones. 'You don't have an automatic right to an explanation, but I'll give you one anyway. Whether you believe it or not is up to you.'

'Can we get out of here first?' Gemma asked on a suddenly shaky note, and saw his jaw tense anew.

'No, we can't! You're not going anywhere till I've finished with you.' He paused briefly, keeping her upright with the same hard grip. 'You left me on deck with Clem, right? It was a good half hour or more before we called it a night. Caryn was waiting for me when I got down to the cabin.'

'That still leaves half an hour,' she said.

'Which it took to convince her there was nothing doing.'

'You could have done that in two minutes!'

'Not with tact and diplomacy.' His mouth was sardonic. 'I perfer to leave illusions intact if at all possible. So far as Caryn is aware, I'm reluctantly compelled to sacrifice my deeper feelings to ambition. In other words, I'm too damned scared of losing Rob's backing to risk making love to his wife, even though I so desperately want to!'

'And she believed it?'

'She wanted to believe it.' His tone had gone flat. 'The way you wanted to believe I invited her down.'

'I didn't want to,' she denied. 'It just—looked

that way.' Despite the warmth of the water she was shivering a little. 'Logan, I——'

'You'd better get to bed,' he said. 'It's going to be light in a couple of hours.'

He was out of the pool and pulling on the silk robe before she reached the top of the ladder. Without speaking, he picked up her own discarded garment and put it about her shoulders. His expression discouraged comment of any kind, but she had to try.

'I'm sorry,' she said. 'I made a mistake.'

The shrug was indifferent. 'We're all entitled.'

Gemma stayed where she was as he moved away, making a production of fastening her belt. Her throat felt as if it were full of sawdust. It was over. It had to be over. Whatever feeling he might have entertained for her, she had killed it stone dead with her hasty assumptions. Well, it solved her other problem anyway. There was no reason now for him ever to know. She would stay aboard and continue to act the part to the best of her ability because she couldn't face the thought of everyone else knowing the truth, but it was going to take every ounce of fortitude she had.

She had to go below eventually, of course. The cabin felt claustrophobic. It took everything she had to close the door and shut herself in. Her hair was too wet to leave. She towelled it roughly, tossing the damp towel over one of the two chairs before taking off her robe and sliding between sheets. The strip light over the bed cast a soft glow she couldn't bear to be without. Two hours to dawn, Logan had said. It was a life sentence.

She was still lying there sleepless when the cabin door opened quietly. Logan came in and closed it again, standing there looking at her with a faint ironic smile on his lips. He was wearing the terry robe provided for all guests on board, his thighs strong and muscular beneath it.

'Want to start again?' he asked. 'From scratch, I mean.'

Gemma came up on one elbow, eyes dark and questioning, heartbeats quickened. 'I'm not sure what that does mean,' she got out. 'Spell it out for me.'

'It's simple enough.' He still didn't move. 'I'm asking you to trust me—to think of me from a new angle. We might not make it, but then again we might just. At least, we can give it a try.'

She didn't have to consider the question; her arms were already stretching out to him. He came into them, passion flaring immediately between them. Never had it been like this before, she thought fleetingly as sense and sanity began to recede. Never in all the world had there been a man more needed than the one now part of her. His name was a shout inside her, ringing in her ears on the long slide down into the bottomless pit.

'Why now?' she was able to whisper some time later when the first madness was past. 'Of all times, why now?'

'Because you're in my blood,' he said, lips at her throat. 'I've always been able to walk away before. This time I'm hooked.'

'For how long?'

'Who can ever tell? Next year we may both feel differently.'

From where she lay, even a year was for ever. The same problems loomed, but she shut them out. Nothing must spoil this moment. Nothing! Logan didn't love her yet, but he was close. By the time she confessed she wanted him to be even closer, their relationship strong enough to survive. A few weeks, that was all she asked. Just a few short weeks!

They had expected to sail before breakfast. Coming aloft to find themselves still anchored in the basin was something of a disappointment to most.

Robert fended off all questions with a smile and a shrug. 'We have another passenger joining us,' he said. 'I only received confirmation at seven. No, I won't tell you who it is. I want it to be a surprise. We sail at midday, all being well.'

Curiosity was rife thoughout the meal, but he refused to drop even a hint. Caryn expressed complete mystification herself. Robert, she said dryly, did not always take her into his confidence.

Whatever her real feelings on the subject, she appeared to have accepted Logan's dismissal without rancour. Gemma had to admire her poise, knowing the struggle she herself would be having right now in the same situation. In deference to the other woman, she tried to avoid catching Logan's eye, too well aware of what one smile of his could do to her facial control. There would be plenty of time later on when they were alone to relive the night they had just spent together. There was time for everything while they were here aboard the *Sea Queen*.

Spiros went across with the launch at eleven. Watching from the rail with the others, Gemma saw the newcomer arrive at the quayside. Judging from the number of trips Spiros made from cab to boat there was a great deal of luggage.

'Has to be a woman,' said Clem on a dry note. 'Trousers or not!'

Whoever she was, her features were too well shaded by the brim of the trilby hat she wore to be seen from a distance. Only when the launch was approaching the yacht did she remove the hat to wave it in greeting, revealing a head of bright red curls and a face familiar enough to draw a concerted breath of recognition from those watching.

'A redheaded Kate!' exclaimed Robert, grinning at the effect his surprise was having. 'Appropriate, wouldn't you say, Logan?'

The younger man was grinning too. 'Very,' he agreed. 'If this means what I think it means, I've got two cats in the bag!'

For the second time in less than twenty-four hours, Gemma was facing a crisis—and not with equanimity either. That was her mother down there. Her mother! How on earth did she get out of this?

There was no way. She had to accept it. Already the launch was coming alongside. Logan moved forward to the head of the gangway to greet his leading lady, taking the slender hand she extended and drawing her forward to kiss her full on the lips.

'Adele! It's been a long time.'

'Too long,' she agreed. The smile lighting her beautifully modelled features embraced the whole company, faltering only as her green eyes came to rest on the girl standing silently by the rail. For a fleeting moment the composure of years was abandoned. 'Gemma? It is you, isn't it?'

In the sudden pause Gemma was conscious of Logan's slow change of expression, of the dawning realisation as he looked from mother to daughter and saw the unmistakable points of resemblance. The hardening of his jawline was an omen for the future. There was steel in the eyes meeting hers.

'We appear to have more than one surprise due,' he said. 'Mine not the least.'

Adele made a fast recovery, the smile returning, if a little over-brightly. 'Darling, what have you been playing at? I thought you were still on the east coast!'

'The show closed because of the weather.' Gemma could see little point in any further prevarication. It was all going to have to come out anyway. She winged a silent appeal in Logan's direction, knowing even as she did so that it was going to be useless asking him to understand her motives. It was too late for the truth. He'd never believe it.

'We have one or two things to discuss,' he said flatly. 'Adele, you'll excuse us?'

'There are one or two questions *I* need to ask, myself,' she responded lightly. 'But I'll give you priority.' She turned the smile on Robert, holding out the same slender hand. 'You're the man I have to thank for this kind invitation, I believe. Such a lovely gesture—and just when I needed the rest!'

Logan waited for Gemma to move, face closed against her. There was a lively speculation in the glances cast her way. Jason looked dumbfounded.

They went below to her cabin. Logan closed the door and leaned against it, reminding her of the night before—except that this time the circumstances did not point towards a happy ending.

'You can start by answering your mother's question,' he said. 'Exactly what *have* you been playing at?'

Gemma sat down on the bed, knees too weak to support her. 'It isn't a game,' she denied. 'Although it might have started out a bit that way. That day you picked me up on the motorway I'd just lost my first job out of theatrical school. I wasn't feeling much like talking about it to anyone.'

'Not even after I'd told you who I was, and what?' He shook his head, answering his own question. 'No, you wouldn't, would you? You were astute enough to realise I'd hardly be tempted to make any concessions for somebody I'd picked up on the road. That offer I made you must have seemed like manna from heaven. An ideal opportunity to prove yourself in a role!' He was speaking in measured tones, his very control an indication of deep-down anger. 'I'll say one thing for you, you put heart and soul into it!'

'You're writing your own script,' she protested. 'It wasn't like that. Not where you—we were concerned.'

'Oh, I see.' There was no give in him. 'Once I exercised my fatal charm you were lost—is that it?'

Gemma ignored the satire, fully aware of the cause. 'I wanted you to make love to me that night,' she said. 'Just as much as you wanted it. I wasn't thinking of anything else at the time.'

'Like hell!' The control was slipping just a

fraction, allowing the hurt to show through. 'You gave the audition of your life that night. I doubt you'll ever better it!'

'Logan.' Her voice was little more than a whisper, her throat too tight to let sound through. 'Don't let it finish because of this. I haven't even thought about an audition since then. I don't even want one. Not if it means losing you.'

'You just lost the lot,' he returned hardily. 'Few people like being made a fool of, Gemma. I'm no exception. What do you think I'm going to tell Rob about all this? Do you really imagine he's going to believe I didn't know who your mother was? I told him we'd been engaged for three months, for God's sake. All right, that makes me a liar too, but at least my reasons were well-intentioned.'

'So well-intentioned you were still seeing his wife behind his back? I saw you together at the theatre, remember?'

'I don't give a damn what you saw, what you thought, or for anything else you might have to say.' The words were clipped. 'If it was ever any of your concern, it certainly isn't now. None of it!'

Pleading with him would be useless, even if she could bring herself to try. This time it really was over. She gathered herself together, putting everything she knew into the philosophical shrug. 'So what happens now? Am I to be despatched forthwith?'

'That's Rob's department,' he came back. 'You're his guest, not mine. I don't imagine he's going to be too hasty when it comes to Adele

Berrisford's daughter. Any blame attached is going to be mine.'

'Your shoulders are broad enough,' she said. 'You'll cope.'

She could see the tensing of muscle beneath the white tee-shirt, hear the hiss of indrawn breath.

'I'd better go,' he said, 'before I come over there and beat the hell out of you. You just don't know when to quit!'

True enough, she thought numbly as the door closed behind him. There was a line beyond which no one should go, and she had crossed it more than once this past week. One week? Was that really all it was? Emotionally she had lived a lifetime.

It took the sound and feel of engines to rouse her from her blank contemplation of the near bulkhead. The clock hands were steady on noon. The cruise was under way. So much for any idea she might have entertained of escape.

Leaving the cabin called for courage, but it had to be faced some time. Gemma found most of the party gathered on the afterdeck to watch the waterfront recede as they headed out for the open sea and the run down to Cape Sounion.

'I'd like to speak to you,' she said to Robert, ignoring—or trying to ignore—the proximity of others. 'I think I owe you a few explanations.'

'You owe *me* a few explanations,' put in her mother, moving to his side. 'It will save time if you tell the story to us both.'

Robert nodded towards the far side of the deck, expression noncommittal. 'Shall we sit down to it?'

Logan was missing, Gemma realised as she followed her mother and host to the indicated spot. If he had already spoken to Robert himself she only hoped he had made a clean breast of everything, because that was what she planned on doing. She had had enough of lies and prevarications.

'Before we start,' said Robert when they were seated, 'I should tell you that Logan made a full confession.' The twinkle in his eyes was spilling over, revealing an amusement he obviously couldn't contain any longer. 'It's the only time I ever had him at a disadvantage. He didn't like it a bit!'

'So what's he doing now?' asked Gemma on a tart note. 'Sulking in his cabin?'

Robert looked at her for a long moment, bringing a flush to her cheeks. 'I think that was a bit uncalled for,' he said mildly. 'You put him in the kind of spot few men would relish.'

'I know.' Her defences had crumbled. She made a small wry gesture. 'It's difficult to explain.'

'Try,' urged Adele, sounding anything but concerned for her daughter's obvious embarrassment. 'I'm beginning to be more and more intrigued by this whole affair. The way you look, for instance. I never realised you had it in you!'

Getting started was the worst part. Told in bare detail, the story took little time to relate.

'What were you doing hitch-hiking in the first place?' asked Adele on an affronted note almost before she had finished. 'I send you enough money, heaven knows!'

'Pride?' suggested Robert. The gaze resting on

Gemma held a certain understanding. 'You'd rather earn what you spend—is that right?'

'These days,' she agreed. She looked at her mother with appeal. 'You've done enough for me. I have to strike out for myself now. I thought if I could just get myself noticed I was in with a chance. If not Bianca then something else.'

Adele laughed. 'Mother and daughter in the same show. Now wouldn't that be something!'

'Yes,' said Robert thoughtfully, 'it certainly would.' His glance went from one face to the other, taking on a growing animation in the process. 'In fact it's too good a notion to pass up. Imagine the publicity! Famous mother, unknown daughter. The public would love it!'

'You're joking!' Adele wasn't laughing any more. 'Darling, few people even know I have a twenty-two-year-old daughter! I'd as soon it stayed that way.'

'Even at the cost of her career?' He shook his head. 'I can't believe Adele Berrisford could ever be that selfish.'

'It isn't selfishness, it's self-preservation,' she denied with some alacrity. 'I was only just eighteen when I had her, but who's going to stop to work that out? They'd tag me with another six or seven years overnight!'

'You could stand it.' Robert was not a man to be worn down by illogical argument, though not above conjuring some of his own. 'You don't look a day over thirty, to start with.'

The famous smile came reluctantly. 'Don't indulge me! I'll settle happily for thirty-five.'

He grinned back. 'Done!'

'Before you go any further,' Gemma put in

levelly, 'you might stop to ask me how I'd feel about it.'

That pulled them up. They turned as one to look at her, surprise plainly written on both countenances. Robert was the first to break the sudden silence.

'I'd have thought you'd grasp the opportunity with both hands. It would be the chance of a lifetime!'

'It hasn't been offered yet,' she pointed out. 'And if it has anything to do with Logan, I doubt if it ever will be.'

'That,' said Robert, 'you can safely leave to me.'

'Meaning you'll only put up the backing if you can dictate the terms?' Gemma shook her head. 'That's hardly playing fair!'

'Since when did a business proposition have to be fair?' he asked, not in the least put out. 'Where hard cash is concerned, I only take calculated risks.'

'You don't even know if I'm capable of taking the part!'

'All right, so we make the deal dependent on your showing.'

'No!' She was trying to stay calm, and not succeeding very well. 'Robert, please don't put me in that position.'

'Darling, you're being very ungrateful,' said Adele reprovingly. 'Don't you have any ambition left?'

'Not if it means using coercion to achieve it.' Gemma paused, searching her mother's face. 'I thought you were against the idea anyway?'

'So far as creating a draw is concerned. I think

my name alone will do that certainly.' The
confidence was not assumed. 'On the other hand,
perhaps Robert is right. I can well afford to cast a
little limelight on my own child.'

'Except that the child doesn't want it.'

'I refuse to believe that,' said Robert with
hardened intonation. 'You're afraid of what
Logan is going to think of you. I may be sticking
my neck out in saying it, but I doubt if it's going
to make a great deal of difference now.'

He was only confirming what Gemma already
knew, yet hearing it put into words made things
infinitely worse. And if they were both right,
what did she have to lose? Her career was all she
had left.

CHAPTER EIGHT

FACING Jason was no easier initially. He listened to what she had to say without comment, shaking his head when she finished.

'I don't pretend to understand you,' he said. 'There were others at the Academy with a parent—or even both—in theatre, but they didn't keep it any secret. Nobody would have thought any worse of you—or any better either, for that matter.'

'There'd have been a difference,' Gemma responded stubbornly. 'Connections gain popularity of a kind I didn't want. My way, I knew the friends I made were genuine.'

'Oh, they were!' He grinned in the familiar, irrepressible fashion. 'Not that I wouldn't have done my damnedest to take advantage anyway if I'd known.' He paused there, studying the profile turned to him as she sat on the edge of his lounger. When he spoke again his tone was gentler. 'How did Logan take it?'

'Predictably.'

'So you're all washed up?'

'Yes.' She clamped down hard on her emotions. 'Only, if your father has anything to do with it, it isn't going to be a clean break. You're not the only condition he's planning on making.'

Brown eyes took on a sharper interest. 'Do tell.'

Gemma explained the situation swiftly and

succinctly, drawing a soft whistle as the implication went home.

'It's some idea!' he said. 'Are you going to go along with it?'

'Why not?' Despite her efforts the bitterness came through. 'It wouldn't be the first deal fixed behind the scenes.'

'Not by a long chalk.' Jason sounded jubilant about it. 'This means the two of us will be dancing together again. Personally, I couldn't ask for better.'

She knew he was serious. Where performance was concerned, Jason suffered no false sentiment. She had on more than one occasion in the past heard him tell people he couldn't work with them because their standards were not his. An egotist maybe, but with some justification. It wasn't for lack of talent that the breaks had not yet come his way. What she must cultivate from now on was the same one-track attitude. Her career had to be everything.

Logan put in an appearance at lunch, outwardly untouched by the events of the morning. On the one occasion when their glances inadvertently crossed, Gemma could read only indifference in his eyes. Whatever she had made him feel for her, it obviously had not gone very deep if he could so swiftly recover from the blow. At least that made her position easier. Concealing her own emotional wretchedness was going to be the most difficult part.

She was grateful for Jason's companionship during the afternoon. The pool was covered while they were at sea, which limited activities to a certain extent, although allowing more deck space. The two of them played quoits for an hour or so, until the heat forced them to take a rest in the shade. Gemma chose a spot as far away as possible from where Logan sat. So far there was no indication that Robert had put his proposition. It would be a bitter pill to swallow, but so would the loss of his main source of finance. He had already committed himself on the basis of it; that much she already knew. With an opening date set, he had little time left in which to find another backer or backers, which would leave him carrying the greater percentage himself. He couldn't afford the luxury of saying no.

Dinner was served in the salon that evening. By common, unspoken consent, everyone dressed for the occasion, although Jason let his side down a little by appearing without jacket or tie—a lack which disturbed him not one iota. Gemma herself had chosen a superbly-cut, utterly unadorned silk sheath the colour of flame. 'Wear this when you feel like making a statement,' Sally had said. Catching Logan's eye as she entered the salon, Gemma knew the message had got across. He would never know what it had cost her.

'You're clashing with my hair,' complained Adele on a semi-serious note. 'Really, darling, I said I didn't mind sharing the limelight, but let's at least do it with harmony!'

From the sudden faint tensing of Logan's jawline, the slip had not gone unnoticed. He was astute enough to put two and two together and come up with the right answer. Gemma saw him glance in Robert's direction, to be met with a bland expression. The latter would choose his own moment to drop his bombshell. Gemma hoped it would not be when she was within earshot.

She made herself think about the advantages of the situation instead. She and Jason would probably be asked to show their paces together as well as separately. They had made a good team in the past; their physical dimensions were sympathetic. They should be capable of tackling anything the choreographer came up with. If she had forfeited Logan's regard in the personal sense, she could at least prove herself to him as an artist.

It was Caryn who suggested a game of bridge. Neither Gemma or Jason were players, which left two of the others high and dry.

'I'd as soon sit out,' claimed Logan. 'Adele and I have a lot to catch up on.'

Caryn's glance switched from his face to that of the other woman in sudden new appraisal. 'I didn't realise you were such old friends!'

'Adele took the lead in my very first production on Broadway five years ago,' he said. 'Without her I'd probably have sunk without trace!'

'So modest, darling!' She was sparkling, well pleased by the compliment. 'We did it together—the two of us! The same way we'll make *Kate* the hit of the century!'

Gemma tore her eyes away, teeth catching at her lower lip. She knew that smile of Logan's: that special, intimate little smile recalling shared moments. Oh God, no, not her mother! Was there any female present he hadn't had?

She had to forcibly remind herself that there were only five years between them. Five years ago it would have seemed even less. She hadn't even known him then, so why let it bother her so much?

She knew why, of course. Five years ago her parents had been divorced. Could Logan have been the cause? Images sprang in her mind's eye: her father's bleak face at the airport the day her mother had left for New York; the silent return to the house they were never again to share as a complete family. No, the split was already begun then. There had been other men; other reasons. None of which helped her accept matters any more easily now. She felt she might choke on the hardness in her throat.

'Take me up on deck, will you?' she murmured to Jason. 'It's stifling in here.'

The air-conditioning was going full blast. He gave her an odd look, but complied readily enough. Gemma doubted if Logan even noted her going. He and her mother were already deep in conversation, the two of them giving the distinct impression that nothing or no one else had any importance.

The night air was balmy, the sea calm enough to make movement easy. Their first port of call was to be Iraklion on the island of Crete, from where they would circle back through the central islands. It was a trip Gemma would once have given a great deal to make. Right now she could conjure up little enthusiasm. She shook her head when Jason offered to send for drinks, relaxing into one of the nearest chairs.

'I just needed to get outside for a while.'

'Away from Logan, you mean?' The pause held significance. 'If you're thinking what I think you are, you're probably right. So what? It isn't as if he knew of the relationship when he met you.'

'Are you sticking up for him?' Gemma asked, and he shrugged.

'Just trying to give you a rational viewpoint. The way you looked at him a few minutes ago you had him down for incest at the very least!'

'See it from my angle,' she said, ignoring the satire. 'How would you feel if you fell for a girl and then found out she'd had an affair with your father?'

'Surprised,' he returned promptly. 'We don't share the same tastes in women either. I like brunettes, he prefers blondes.'

'Jason!'

'Okay!' He spread his hands in mock repentance. 'So I might not like it. That doesn't mean I'd make myself miserable over it. Especially where I'd already finished with the girl in question. You're going to have to get yourself sorted out if you want to make it through the audition. The last thing you're going to need is an emotional problem!'

He was only telling her what she knew already to be true. Logan wasn't the only man in the world. Forget him. If she did get the part they would only be involved so far as the show itself was concerned, and that in the barest of senses. So be it, she thought in sudden resolve.

Having no desire to return to the salon, Gemma elected to go straight to her cabin when they did finally leave the deck. At a little after eleven-fifteen it felt too early to retire for the night. She listened to the radio for a while, and tried to interest herself in a book without a great deal of success. Eventually she gave in and began to prepare for the night.

Each single cabin had its own shower and toilet adjoining. She was rinsing herself beneath a final cool needle spray, her back to the curtain, when the water was suddenly turned off and the towelling robe thrust roughly about her shoulders.

'Come out!' commanded Logan. He sounded grim.

Gemma obeyed. There was little choice. He was capable of dragging her out by brute force if necessary. He returned to the main cabin to wait for her as she seized a small towel to wrap about her wet hair. When she went through he was standing with hands thrust deep into the pockets of his dress trousers, the white tuxedo tossed over the nearby chair.

'Stripped for action?' she asked with deliberate flippancy. 'What did you have in mind?'

'A few home truths for starters,' he came back. 'Adele tells me there's no way you could have known she had been approached about playing Kate, which means the idea had to come to you on the spur of the moment. You're quick to see an advantage, I'll grant you that. It's exactly the kind of calculated gimmick Rob would go for!'

Gemma's brows had knotted. 'I'm not sure I understand.'

'You to play Bianca to your mother's Kate.' The grey eyes were narrowed and hard. 'You're not trying to deny the suggestion came from you?'

So that was it! She should have known, Gemma reflected with irony. Her mother had always been adept at what the Americans would call 'passing the buck'. In all probability she had actually persuaded both herself and Robert that the suggestion had indeed originated from her daughter. Denying it was a waste of time. It hardly mattered anyway. Logan's opinion of her was already set.

'You have to admit it has its possibilities,' she responded. 'You're going to need some good publicity to cancel out the memory of last year's short run.'

'Last year I made the mistake of thinking unknowns could carry the show. This year I have Berrisford and Sullivan as leads. That's a combination that can't fail.'

'But you still have to fill the supporting roles.' She had the robe belted tightly about her, her crossed arms hugging her waist as if in support. 'Did you have anyone in mind for Bianca?'

'The choice was to be made via open audition. Now I'm supposed to go back there and tell my director I've already cast two vital roles without even consulting him?'

So Jason was definitely involved. Gemma scarcely knew what she felt any more. Logan was right, the whole thing was underhand, yet it wouldn't be by any means the first time it had happened. It had long been said in the theatre world that it wasn't so much a case of what you could do, but of being in the right place at the right time and knowing the right people. She would be an idiot not to take advantage of those very circumstances right now.

'Robert agreed to let the decision rest on my showing,' she said. 'I imagine he'll apply the same ruling to Jason. At least give us both the chance to prove ourselves. We've danced together before.'

His lip curled. 'Vertically too?'

Gemma was unable to control the angry flush running under her skin. 'Get out!' she clipped. 'I don't have to take that from you!'

He didn't move. 'If you go through with this you'd better steel yourself, because there's a lot more where that came from.'

'Oh, I can imagine!' She was hurting too much to heed the danger signals in his eyes. 'Your pride's been punctured and you can't take it. Not when it's someone you thought you had right under your thumb that's done the puncturing! You were willing enough to use *me*. Why take exception when I return the compliment? Or does it go deeper than that perhaps? Does the fact that you've been involved with my mother in the past make you feel guilty?'

'Guilty of what?' The skin about his mouth was white.

'Call it what you like. I know what the press would make of it if they ever got hold of it!'

'And if I decide to back off from Rob's deal you might just consider giving it to them, is that it?'

It wasn't. She had been talking for the sake of talking, trying to trick him into an admission that would settle any last lingering doubt in her mind. Faced with a direct question, she could go only one way.

'Why not? Think of the publicity angle. The term 'family man' would take on a whole new concept!'

It was a full ten seconds before he moved: Gemma knew that because she found herself mentally counting. When he did start for her he seemed almost in slow motion, his every step taken with such conscious purpose.

She backed at the same speed, coming up against the bulkhead in short order. Oddly enough there was no fear in her, just the heart-thudding awareness of what was to happen.

The fingers fastening on to her shoulders were like steel, his mouth cruel. She made a faint and involuntary sound of protest swiftly squashed beneath the relentless pressure, feeling his hands move downwards inside the bathrobe to bring her up hard against him. There was no escaping that strength of his; she wasn't even sure she wanted to escape it. Any emotion was better than none.

It was Logan himself who called a halt, breath coming short and heavy as he lifted his head.

'No,' he gritted. 'This is one time we leave it right here! You'll get your chance. You and Jason both. Only you'd better make the most of it, because there'll just be the one. Fail, and the whole lot of you can go to hell!'

Gemma stood rigidly against the bulkhead as he snatched up the tuxedo and left. Only after the door was safely closed did she relax her locked knees and slide slowly to a sitting position on the floor. Robert had won after all. She was to have her opportunity to prove herself. The fact that she would cheerfully renounce all claim just to have Logan back again was totally by the way.

They reached Crete some time during the night, awakening to a coastal view of pure white sand backed by low hills and a forest of palms.

'Just an hour from Iraklion,' Robert informed them at breakfast. 'One of the finest beaches for miles. I thought we might spend the morning here, then head for port after lunch. Agreed?'

'You're the organiser,' said Logan shortly. 'Speaking personally, there are a dozen other things I could be doing right now.'

'We'll talk about it later over a drink,' came the unmoved reply. 'Just for now, relax, man! You don't do enough of it.'

'He never did,' put in Adele with the air of one who should know. 'Gemma darling, Logan tells me you and Jason are to audition when we get back to London. I hope you both of you realise how very lucky you are. It isn't often an opportunity like this comes along.'

'When Robert takes a hand, anything can happen,' said Caryn unemotionally. 'I'm only just beginning to realise that myself.' She pushed back her chair and stood up, not even glancing in Robert's direction. 'I'm going to change for the beach. Spiros will be rowing me across in about fifteen minutes, if anyone else is interested. He can always make more than one journey.'

'Or we can always break out a dinghy.' Robert's tone was dry. He crumbled a piece of bread between his fingers as his wife walked away without answering, glancing round the assembled party with a brief shrug. 'A slight marital disagreement—nothing of importance. If everyone is of the same mind I'll organise the transport. Pity we couldn't stow the launch. It would have speeded things up.'

There was a pause after he had gone. Predictably, Adele was the first to break it. 'The problem with so many marriages is lack of give and take,' she sighed.

'The problem with some marriages is when one partner does all the giving and the other the taking,' responded Clem on an unusually cynical note for him.

'You're not including us in there, I hope?' said his wife, and drew a smile.

'You know I'm not. We've too much in common.'

Including age, reflected Gemma. Perhaps if she found a man closer to her own she stood a chance of a happy relationship.

She was kidding herself and she knew it. It was Logan's maturity which had attracted her to him in the first place. He had spoiled her for younger men.

They all went across to the beach in the end. Spiros showed a marked reluctance to leave them. Only when Ida Rourke appeared on deck to shout his name through cupped hands did he climb disconsolately back into the boat.

'Poor Spiros.' Beryl exclaimed in sympathy. 'Having to work on a day like this! Plus four more journeys to make to get us all back on board again when the time comes.'

'It's what he's here for,' said Robert without lifting his head from its supine position. 'The job's a sinecure for a boy his age. Come the end of the season, he'll have more drachmas in his pocket than he ever had in his life before.'

'Come and swim,' Jason invited Gemma. 'The water's clear as crystal. Just out to the rocks there. That shouldn't tax your strength too much.'

She rose to the challenge, striking out from the beach for the tiny islet at the mouth of the cove. Jason finished half a length in front of her, dragging himself from the water to sprawl on bare rock.

'I'd say we should start some regular limbering-up sessions,' he stated when he had recovered his breath. 'A weeks' idleness and I'm as stiff as a board!'

Gemma could only agree. Her own muscles ached far more than they should. 'Where and how?' she asked.

'On deck, early morning—where else? The cabins aren't big enough to rig a practice barre. Six o'clock, then we'll have it to ourselves. Think you can manage it?'

'No problem.' It would be a relief, she reflected, to have some definite aim instead of lying awake thinking of things she would as soon forget. 'Starting tomorrow?'

'Right.' Jason rolled over on to his side, allowing his eyes to drift the length of her body. 'You know, you've altered in more ways than one. You haven't put any weight on, yet you seem more—I don't know—womanly, I suppose.'

'It's the weight of years,' she said. 'All twenty-two!' She stiffened at the touch of his hand, opening her eyes on blinding blue sky. 'Don't,' she whispered. 'Jason, I——'

The hand was withdrawn immediately. He turned on his back again. For a moment or two he was silent. When he did speak it was on a note of impatience. 'What are you going to do—spend the rest of your life in solitary? He's one man, for God's sake!'

'I know.' Her voice was husky. 'And I'll get over him. Only not too soon, and not——'

'And not with me,' he finished for her. 'Okay, I can accept that. Just kick yourself back into top gear. You're going to need every bit of get up and go you've got to play Bianca—unless the part's been written down for Telford's production.'

Gemma was sitting up now, picking minute particles of sand from the rock surface. 'No, it hasn't. I've seen the score. All the big numbers are there. Jean Scott is choreographer.'

'Right. I've done some homework too. One of the few who'll go along with individual inter-pretation, providing it doesn't clash too hard with her own ideas. I'm going to enjoy working with her. So are you.' His tone was resolute. 'We'll make it through!' He stood up, body supple as a willow. 'See you back on the beach.'

Gemma stayed where she was as he dived into the water. There was no rush. They were to lunch right here on the beach before returning to the yacht for the cruise round the headland to Iraklion. Robert had planned on a two-night stay: he had even reserved berthing space in advance. It was not for want of forethought that the trip was proving rather less than the delight it should have been.

From where she sat she could view the whole party spread over the white sand. Caryn had her back turned towards her husband who was talking with Logan and Adele, her very posture indicative of her frame of mind. Gemma wondered how much longer the marriage could last. Caryn was young enough and beautiful enough to find any number of rich men willing to keep her in the manner to which she was accustomed. What she might never find again was one capable of loving her the way Robert loved her.

Of all the females in the party, probably Beryl was the only one who knew what contentment really meant. Gemma found her easy to be with; she fancied Clem did too. Lying sunbathing side by side, the two of them looked companionable even from here.

Bright red curls caught the sunlight as Adele threw back her head to laugh, the sound trilling across the water. Logan had an arm draped lightly across her shoulders, his smile reflecting her amusement. Gemma watched with pain in her heart. She had to become accustomed to thinking of Logan as lost to her, but it didn't help to see him with her mother. While he had not actually admitted to any previous intimacy between them he hadn't denied it either. Looking at them now she could only believe it had to be true. And what had happened five years ago could well happen again. Almost certainly her mother would feel no compunction about it. In fact she might even regard it as a feather in her cap to steal a man from her daughter!

Except that it wouldn't be stealing, Gemma was bound to acknowledge. That implied ownership on her part. Logan was a free agent; he always would be a free agent. She could find some comfort in the thought that breaking up was easier now than it would have been six months or a year hence, mother or no mother.

Lunch was in progress when she finally swam back to the beach, the food and wine kept beautifully cool and fresh in the refrigerated carriers. With a chicken drumstick in one hand and a glass in the other, Gemma wandered a little way up the beach to find some shade beneath a palm, tucking herself down on the far side of one of the larger boles. She had never been a solitary person, but she felt one today. It was just a case of getting hold of herself: tomorrow she would face the world with equanimity. A few hours wasn't much to ask.

After the heat and the exercise it was probably inevitable that she should fall asleep. She awoke what seemed like bare moments later to find both drumstick and glass half buried in the sand by her knee, and alive with ants.

Only as she leapt hurriedly to her feet did the silence penetrate. Not a total silence by any means: the calling of birds, the humming of insects, the breaking of waves on the shore; they were all there. What she missed was the sound of voices. Which was hardly surprising, she discovered on stepping out from behind the palm. The beach was deserted, the yacht itself vanished from its anchorage, the wide blue sea beyond empty of life.

With her watch left back on the yacht for safety's sake, she had no means of knowing exactly how long she had slept, and at this latitude the sun was little help. Her first reaction was sheer indignation that the rest of the party could have returned on board without even noticing her absence, an emotion soon overtaken by concern as her predicament became clearer. Disregarding the whys and wherefores of her abandonment, she had spent most of the morning showing a marked preference for her own company, and been allowed to indulge it. If no one knew she wasn't on board then how long was it going to be before her absence was discovered?

It was a long and lonely afternoon. From sitting on the edge of the beach gazing hopefully seaward, Gemma graduated to considering the possibility of making her own way to Iraklion. Her study of the island map on display the previous evening had been cursory to say the least, but she recalled a road skirting the northern coastline. If she could make her way to it she could perhaps hitch a lift into town.

Common sense knocked that idea on the head almost as it took shape. Even if she could find the road there may be little traffic. Neither was she dressed for any such attempt. Hitching lifts was the root cause of all her problems: one was supposed to profit from one's mistakes not compound them. Sooner or later someone was going to question her non-appearance, and then steps would be taken. Until then the only thing she could safely do was wait.

She heard the speedboat before she saw it, coming swiftly to her feet as the streamlined white craft curved the headland. Only when the engine power was reduced to allow the boat to drift in on tick-over did she recognise the man behind the wheel. Whatever the emotions expressed in the set of his features, concern was not among them.

'Get in!' he called, turning the wheel to bring him sideways on to where she stood. 'I don't want to beach her.'

And that was to be it? No apology, no word of comfort, just the terse command anticipating instant compliance. Something snapped deep inside, flooding her with an anger that tremored every limb. If the blame for this fiasco was to be hers, then let him have something to blame her for!

He let out a shout as she turned and began to walk away up the beach. 'Gemma! What the devil?——'

The gunning of the engine drowned anything else he might have said. She didn't care if he was leaving her. Let him go! They could send someone else to fetch her. Someone who might give a thought to what she had been going through these past hours.

The engine note died completely; she heard the grating sound as fibreglass slid over gritty sand, followed by the splash of feet through the shallows. Still she refused to turn round, gripped by a compulsion she couldn't have explained to anyone, and made any sense.

Logan caught her just within the fringe of the trees, whipping her round with a hand like iron.

'What kind of crazy game are you playing?' he demanded harshly. 'Have you any idea of the trouble you've caused?'

Trouble *she* had caused! She struck out blindly, seeing the red mark appear as if by magic down one lean cheek, the sudden savage blaze in his eyes.

This time there was no backing off on his part.

His weight bore her down into the sand. Gemma responded with the same raw fury, fighting like a wild thing until his superior strength got the upper hand. Only then did the anger in her alter character, her body softening beneath him, opening to take him into her; wrapping him in silken limbs. The sun was a flickering light through the palm fronds, green merging with gold into one dazzling burst of colour before fading slowly away to misty nothing.

He would never forgive her this either; she knew that at once. She had caused him to lose control with a totality his male pride alone would be unable to accept. It was what she had wanted, yet it gave her little satisfaction now it was done.

Logan had himself well in hand by the time he did roll away from her. His face was expressionless.

'I'll be down at the boat when you're ready,' he said after he got to his feet. 'It's going to be dark pretty soon, and I'm not familiar with the coastline.'

Gemma had to force the words out. 'Logan, wait a minute!'

He paused but didn't turn, his stance unrelenting. 'For what?'

'Everything.' It hurt to talk. 'Why did you come back for me?'

'Because I'm responsible for your being here in the first place.' He was moving again as he spoke, not looking back. 'Just get yourself together.'

The boat was already afloat when she reached the water's edge. Logan gave her an impersonal hand in climbing aboard, then hoisted himself over the side to slide behind the wheel.

'It's going to be noisy,' he said, 'so we'll get the explanations over now. We split into two parties coming over, if you remember. We did the same going back. Rob and your mother and I were the last to leave. We'd been talking when the others went, and just took it for granted you'd gone with them. They took it equally for granted you'd be coming with us. Considering the way you'd been acting, we all accepted that you'd decided to stay in your cabin for the afternoon. It wasn't until Jason went down to see what was eating you, after we got to Iraklion, that anybody realised you weren't even on board.' The shrug was not apologetic. 'All's well that ends well. Maybe next time you'll tell someone before you wander off.'

'I didn't wander off,' Gemma admitted. 'I fell asleep behind that big palm back there.'

'It must have been a very deep sleep.'

'I had a bad night.' She hesitated, glancing at the hard-cut profile. 'Logan, what happened just now——'

'Won't be happening again,' he slid in hardily. 'Leave it alone, will you.'

'I can't,' she said. 'If you'd only——'

'I said leave it!' He hadn't raised his voice, but the tone silenced her. 'Just for once in your life have the sense to back off!'

A flick of one lean brown wrist brought the engine to life with a roar of sound. Gemma sat back defeatedly in her seat as he opened the throttle and headed out to sea. She had left the wine glass behind, came the irrelevant thought. One thing was certain, they would not be coming back for it.

CHAPTER NINE

DARKNESS was on them a good fifteen minutes before they reached the safety of the harbour. Logan brought them in slowly and carefully by the light of the stars, rounding the forbidding ramparts of the Venetian fortress to come alongside the quay behind *Sea Queen*.

'You'd better get on board and put their minds at rest while I return this to its owner,' he said, leaning out to grasp one of the mould-covered iron rings let into the stonework and pull the boat into line with the steps. 'Look slippy—I can't hold us here all night!'

Gemma did so, glad to be back on dry land again. Her hair was wet from the spray of their passage, her limbs chilled by the wind of it. She didn't wait to see Logan pull away again.

Jason was down the gangway before she reached it, slinging one of the towelling robes about her shoulders.

'Thought you might need this,' he said. 'You had everybody going spare when we realised what must have happened. Dad wanted to turn the yacht round, but Logan beat him to it. He'd hired that speedboat and taken off before anybody else got past talking about it.'

'Where are they all?' Gemma asked, glancing up at the deck as she mounted the gangway ahead of him.

'Keeping out of sight until they can face you *en*

masse, I shouldn't wonder.' Jason's tone was wry. 'We're all feeling a bit cut up over leaving you behind like that. No excuses are adequate.'

'It was as much my fault as anyone's,' she denied, warmed already by the show of concern. 'Personally, I'd as soon forget it.'

'I'll pass the message on. Your mother will be relieved. I don't think she could make up her mind which way to play the homecoming scene—especially after Logan pulled her up for laying the blame on you.'

Gemma made no comment. Her mother wasn't the only player of parts on board this boat. Not by a long way!

'Are you going to feel up to dining out?' asked Jason when they were below deck. 'Or would you rather call it a day? I don't mind staying on board to keep you company.'

'Thanks,' she said softly, 'but I'm perfectly okay. At least I shall be after I get cleaned up. What time do we go?'

'Oh, you've got another hour. Don't bother dressing up. Dad knows this local *kendro* where they do the authentic Greek dancing for later on. None of this tourist stuff for him.'

'He's obviously been here before.'

'So have I. We came to the islands a couple of times a year when my mother was alive.' He paused at her cabin door, glancing at her face. 'You look all in. Sure you don't want to change your mind?'

'Quite sure. I'll see you on deck.'

It was a relief to be alone again. Gemma took a few moments to gather herself before beginning to consider what she was going to wear.

Something simple, Jason had intimated. Her white cotton pants and halter top should fit the bill. But first a shower to get rid of the sand.

She was ready in less than half an hour, her hair shampooed and blow-dried to a smoothly shining helmet. The white pants fitted snugly, outlining the shape of hip and leg. It was a dancer's body she saw in the mirror, slender and lissom, her skin tanned to a pale shade of gold. Little else about her remained unchanged.

Waiting until she imagined everyone else would be gathered aft for pre-dinner drinks, she went to join them, weathering the chorus of exclamations, questions and faintly defensive statement with a smile and a shrug.

'Don't worry, I'll be sticking close in future!'

'It was the shock,' said her mother, unwilling to let the subject drop. 'For all we knew you could have fallen overboard!'

Logan laughed, taking the hand resting on the chair arm between them and putting it lightly to his lips. 'You're dramatising, darling!'

'Well, perhaps just a little.' She sparkled to the attention. 'If you ever have a child of your own you'll understand the worry they can be.'

Since when? wondered Gemma. Even as a small child she had learned to look to her father for parental guidance, for the simple reason that her mother was so rarely available. She caught Jason's swift wink, and made herself relax. He was right. Let it go over her head. Her mother couldn't help the way she was. If Logan chose to indulge her that was his affair. She was, after all, his leading lady.

They ate at Limni's on the inner harbour,

sticking for the most part to seafood and salad. Afterwards, they all piled into a couple of hired cars for the drive to the inland village where the rest of the evening's entertainment was to take place.

The village itself was off the beaten track, and tiny, consisting of one surfaced main street with a couple of bars and a shop. A huddle of white-walled houses climbed the hillside. The whole populace appeared to be gathered at the *kendro* right out on the far side, music and voices mingling on the air. Adele turned up her nose a little on first sight of the crowded bench-like tables set down both sides of an open courtyard. Drinks were being served from a rough stone building to the rear.

Robert greeted several people by name, and was embraced with enthusiasm in return. Somehow room was made for them all to sit down. The two musicians playing the traditional *bouzouki* struck up another of the plaintive tunes: immediately the whole group of young men got up and clasped arms to form a circle, moving with surprising grace through the series of simple steps which formed the dance.

Shirt and slacks appeared to be the general male uniform. Only among the women was there any noticeable effort towards individuality, each colourful dress vying with its neighbour. Gemma tried out her few words of Greek on the elderly woman sitting opposite, and was rewarded with a beaming smile and a whole torrent in reply. Laughing, she was forced to indicate that she couldn't understand. It seemed to make little difference to the atmosphere.

For the most part, dancing seemed to be an activity confined to the men. During the following couple of hours the women got up only when a guitarist took over from the *bouzouki* players for a short session of popular numbers even the English could recognise. Gemma was asked to dance by a dark-eyed Lothario who spent the whole of it breathing heavily in her ear. 'The language of love!' murmured Jason on her return to the table. 'We could feel him smouldering from here!'

Gemma could feel Logan's eyes on her, but she refused to glance his way, too sure of what she would see in them. Let him use up his mockery somewhere else!

As if to confound former impressions, the very next Greek number had a girl and boy performing the steps alone together. Jason watched with critical eye.

'We could do that,' he said *sotto voce* to Gemma as the pair finished to enthusiastic applause. 'In fact why not? It's high time we showed this lot what we're made of!'

He was gone before Gemma could stop him, crossing the dirt floor to talk to the musicians. She went hot and then cold as he gesticulated in her direction. No! He wouldn't!

But he had. Somebody caught the gist of his meaning and passed it on to a neighbour. Like a breeze through grass, the whisper went round, drawing indulgent smiles along with the nods and cries of encouragement. The *Anghlos* were going to show them how to dance. How droll!

Gemma shook her head as Jason beckoned her, hanging on to her poise by the skin of her teeth.

If he was so desperate to dance he could do it alone!

'You'll have to go,' Robert advised with some sympathy. 'That son of mine has just issued a challenge he isn't going to be allowed to retract.'

'Think of it as upholding the flag,' drawled Caryn. Her eyes held a glint of malice. 'After all, you're both trained dancers. These poor souls are mere amateurs!'

There was no help from Logan's direction either. He wasn't even looking her way. Gemma steeled herself to get to her feet, forcing a smile for all the watching eyes. She would do something drastic to Jason for this later; for the moment she had no choice.

He met her halfway, grinning confidently. 'Stop being defeatist,' he told her. 'We'll slay 'em!'

'I don't even know the steps!' she hissed.

'I do. Just follow me. When you've got the feel we'll improvise a little.'

It was hopeless arguing. All she could do was go along, and hope for the best. Jason took her hand as the music began, lifting it high between them and poising his other hand for balance. Automatically Gemma copied him, coming on to the balls of her feet to take the first slow step in his wake. One-two-together; one-two-together: left foot behind, transfer the weight, down and glide and repeat. Nothing difficult there. So far, so good.

The tension left her as the rhythm caught her up. Effortlessly, faultlessly, she followed her partner's guide, widening the scope and quickening the pace as the musicians responded to the invitation in Jason's laughing gesture; building to a climax which left all four of them breathless and grinning like fools to the shouts and cheers of an appreciative audience.

'You just put Anglo-Greek relations up another notch,' Robert commented when they returned to the table. 'You can't say they don't make a good pair, Logan.'

'Hardly.' The other man's tone was cool. 'The deal's already made. All they have to do is convince both director and choreographer they can handle the numbers. You're due back in London a week Wednesday. I'll set things up for the Friday.'

'You're going back before us?' Gemma tried to keep her tone casual.

'I'm flying out from here in the morning,' he said.

'Oh, what a shame!' exclaimed Beryl with genuine regret. 'You've hardly been away five minutes!'

Adele wore a bright smile. 'I did consider going with him, but I can't bear to tear myself away from such wonderful hospitality!'

'Thanks.' Caryn made no attempt to disguise the irony. 'We do our best. Is everyone ready to go back to the yacht?'

It was difficult getting away because so many insisted on saying a personal goodbye. By the time they got into the cars again it was gone eleven-thirty. Only the men were prepared to take up Robert's suggestion of a nightcap when they finally reached the boat, the women preferring to call it a day.

Alone at last, Gemma went over to her bedside

locker and took out the cream leather box containing the diamond ring. She should have returned it before this, but finding the right moment had been proving difficult. It was going to be even more difficult now, yet it had to be done. She only had tonight.

At least she could rest easy in the knowledge that her mother wasn't going with him. She even had the impression that he had been the one to scotch the idea. If he was going to be busy distraction of that kind was the last thing he was going to need.

She kept her mind on totally inconsequential matters while she waited for the faint sounds that would tell her someone had entered the cabin beyond the rear bulkhead, counting the rivets around the porthole, the grid holes in the air vent—anything rather than think what life was going to be like once Logan had gone. The coming days were going to be the longest she had ever spent in her life.

It seemed long enough before she heard what she was listening for. All was quiet in the alleyway when she left her cabin to make her way round to the other door. Logan answered her soft knock almost immediately, his face undergoing a fleeting change of expression before closing up again. Gemma held out the ring box.

'I only came to bring you this. You'll need to get it back to the jewellers.' She drew in a painfully tight breath. 'Goodbye, Logan. I'm sorry for not being honest with you. It all got away from me.'

She was already turning to go when he said her name, his tone unemotional.

'We can't just leave it like this. Come on in for a moment.'

Her hesitation was not calculated. 'I don't think there's much point.'

'There is if we're to part without any more misunderstandings.' He held open the door a little wider. 'Just one or two things I need to say. It won't take long.'

Gemma went because she couldn't help herself, facing him as he closed the door again. He was still fully dressed in the light-coloured slacks and shirt, the latter unfastened at the wrists as if he had begun to remove it at the moment she knocked. The longing to be in his arms tore at her throat.

'About your mother,' he said, not coming any closer. 'You were wrong, Gemma. We were never lovers. I should have made it clear last night when you threw it at me.'

She believed him instantly and relief flooded her. 'I'm glad,' she said. 'I should have known.'

'Oh, not because the thought never crossed my mind,' he admitted with a wry twist of his lips. 'I used to have a golden rule—never mix business with pleasure. I break it once, and look what happens!'

'You're landed with an arrangement you'd never have accepted without coercion.' Gemma paused, forcing herself to say it. 'Would it help at all if I backed out?'

Grey eyes narrowed as if trying to read her mind. 'You'd do that?'

'I wouldn't want to.' She had to be honest. 'Chances don't come all that easily. I didn't agree with the way Robert handled things though. I still don't.'

'But you still went along.'

'What else was left?' In spite of her desperate need to control it, her voice had a tremor in it. 'I was willing to give it all up if we could just have gone on the way we were. I was telling you the truth when I said I hadn't even thought about my career in days. The other night you said you'd always been able to walk away before, but you couldn't from me. Has all that gone completely?'

'No.' His own voice was suddenly rough. 'Wasn't that what you set out to prove this afternoon?'

'I'm not sure what I was trying to prove this afternoon.' She made a small movement towards him, her eyes searching his face for some faint sign of softening. 'Logan?'

'It wouldn't work,' he said. 'It probably never would have. The gap is too wide.'

'You mean age?'

He slanted a smile. 'Not entirely, although it does have some bearing. You'd expect too much from me, Gemma. I'm not cut out for marriage and children and living happily ever after!'

'What makes you so sure I am?'

'If you're not that way inclined now you will be eventually. I can sense it in you.'

'If you can sense that much you must know how I feel about you,' she said desperately. 'I don't care about the future. I care about now! Take me back with you tomorrow.'

He shook his head. 'I'm going to be too tied up to have you on my hands.' There was a pause before he added on a softer note, 'If you're going back to your cabin you'd better go now.'

Gemma knew what he was offering her: one

more night together with no strings attached. She knew she should refuse, but she couldn't bring herself to do it. If nothing else, she could leave him with a memory of her that wouldn't jar.

Wakening at five still wrapped together like Siamese twins was no new experience. For a fleeting moment or two, Gemma actually thought they were in bed at the Thames studio, until the comparative narrowness of the mattress brought her back to earth.

In a few hours Logan would be away. If she followed him she could only be creating problems for them both. Yet after this night they had just passed, he surely couldn't intend the parting to be final. It had been heaven; and not just for her.

He awoke with his usual instant recall, smiling into her eyes. His jaw was rough, but she was used to that too. When he kissed her she responded without thinking about it, reaching for him with avid hands.

He rolled, pulling her on top of him, watching her face as she pressed herself upright, his hands tracing the line of her body as if painting a picture in his mind's eye. Then they were settling on her hips and she was moving to his urging, faster and wilder until thought and feeling merged into one pulsing beat and the world collapsed about their heads.

'You'd better get back to your cabin while it's still quiet,' he suggested around six. He kissed her temple softly, then got out of bed himself, reaching for the silk dressing gown. 'I need to be at the airport by nine.'

There was little point in asking if she could see

him off. Gemma doubted if she could take it anyway. Their goodbyes had to be said here and now.

'What happens when I get back?' she asked huskily, and he turned to glance at her.

'I already said I'd set things up.'

'I'm not talking about the show, I'm talking about us. Don't I even get to see you on a personal basis?'

There was a pause before he answered, his expression wryly resigned. 'Under the circumstances it's probably best if we don't meet outside the theatre.'

'I may not get the part.'

He smiled. 'You'll get it. You and Jason both. You're natural partners. Add the publicity incentive and no director could fail to be swayed.'

'Unless he just happened to have someone picked out himself.'

'Then I'd have to overrule him. Which is one more reason why I don't want any gossip about the two of us.' He was speaking with precision, tidying up all the loose ends. 'I'll fix you up with somewhere to live until you're on your feet—assuming you'll not be sharing a hotel suite with your mother?'

Gemma shook her head. 'She wouldn't want that any more than I would. And I'd rather find my own place to live.'

'Using the money Adele's been sending you? I was under the impression you didn't want to touch that.'

'I didn't—I don't.' She stopped, recognising the futility. 'I can always pay it back.'

'Whereas you don't think I'd take it.' He

shrugged noncommitally. I'll check if Sally still has the flat going free over the shop.'

Gemma let the matter rest there. It would be stupid to turn down that offer too. Accommodation was not easy to find. Logan had placed his bathrobe ready for her on the bed. She got up and pulled it on, avoiding his eyes as she tightened the belt.

'I'll bring it back later,' she said, picking up the clothing she had so eagerly discarded. 'It wouldn't do for Mrs Rourke to find them both in the same cabin.'

'I don't imagine she'd consider it her business.' Logan came and drew her round to face him, finding her mouth in a kiss that held regret. 'I'm going to miss you, Gemma.'

But not for long, she thought miserably. He would find someone else, the way he always had. Had she been vindictive she would have wished that he would one day feel the way she did right now about someone, and be as helpless to do anything about it, only that kind of spite was beyond her. She would find someone else too eventually, and all this would fade into the past. Time dulled even the most vivid memories, it was said. She had to hope that was true.

She left him packing, making her way back to her own cabin without seeing a soul. A shower refreshed her body if not her emotions. The light knocking came on her door just as she finished pulling on shorts and top. Jason stood in the alleyway.

'I thought I heard water running,' he said. 'I tried earlier, but you must have been asleep. Are you ready?'

'For what?' asked Gemma, unable to make her brain function at anything like its normal speed. 'It's only about half past six!'

'Our exercise session,' he responded. 'Don't tell me you'd forgotten already!'

'I'm afraid I had,' she confessed.

'Oh, well, no harm done. We still have plenty of time before breakfast.' Jason waited until she had joined him in the alley before adding curiously, 'If you'd forgotten our arrangement, what were you doing up so early anyway?'

'I couldn't sleep,' she said, stepping on ahead of him. 'Perhaps it was my subconscious prodding me. What are we going to use as a barre?'

'Rope,' he replied promptly. 'I've already rigged it up good and taut and at the right height. We can take it down again when we're through.'

The morning was delicious, the view out over the city to the low hills sparklingly clear. Gemma poured every ounce of concentration into the following hour, groaning as she brought into play muscles unused for too long.

'An hour a morning isn't really long enough,' Jason declared at the end of it when they both sprawled exhausted on the nearest loungers.

'It's better than nothing.' Gemma forced herself to her feet. 'I'm going to have to wash my hair. It's soaked!'

Logan and Robert came out on deck as she approached the double doors leading below. The former was carrying his suitcase and wearing the same slacks and light jacket in which he had travelled just three days ago. Gemma kept right on going, the smile fixed to her lips.

'No breakfast?' she queried.

'I'll pick something up at the airport,' Logan replied. 'It's going to be a full flight. I don't want to get bumped.'

'That looks like the taxi arriving,' said Robert, nodding down at the quay. 'I'll go and secure it.'

'You don't need to be tactful,' the younger man cut in dryly. 'Gemma and I have already said our goodbyes.' His smile touched her lightly. 'Take care. We'll see you on stage.'

We, not I. He was making sure she understood the position. Last night might not have happened, for all the feeling in his voice. He nodded to Jason behind her. 'You too. Keep up the practice.'

Gemma carried on below as he moved off in the direction of the gangway. Watching him actually leave would be more than she could bear.

Breakfast was served in the salon for once. Adele heard of Logan's departure with unconcealed indignation.

'He could at least have waited to say goodbye!' she exclaimed.

'He'll be seeing you again in less than a fortnight,' said Robert consolingly. 'I expect he thought it was hardly worthwhile. He did say to tell you to take it easy. He needs you.'

'He needs my box-office pull,' she retorted with more than a hint of asperity. Her eyes went to her daughter's face, hardening a fraction more in the process. 'And I'll be supplying it—with or without the gimmicks!'

Gemma met her gaze without flinching. 'That goes without saying. You're the star. You were always meant to be a star. You sing, and I dance. There's no competition.'

Adele laughed. 'Between mother and daughter, darling, there's always competition! You're costing me several years I'd prefer to keep to myself a while longer—at least so far as my public image is concerned. Forty is a difficult enough age for a woman to face as it is, without having it added to. You wait and see!'

Another eighteen years. Where would she be then? Gemma wondered. If success came, would it be worth all the heartache? What did her mother really have, when it came right down to it? To be so afraid of growing older must surely colour one's whole existence.

CHAPTER TEN

HAD it not been for Jason and his insistence that they work out at every available opportunity, Gemma doubted if she could have got through the rest of the cruise. The islands they visited blurred in her mind until she was no longer sure which scenic memory was which. Only when they were on the last lap back to Piraeus did she begin to regret her lack of interest in places she would be unlikely ever to see again.

There was a telegram waiting when they docked. She tore it open with eager fingers, her heart sinking at the brevity of the message contained. Accommodation with Sally was arranged and the private auditions set for Friday morning at ten. Obviously Logan was not planning any kind of meeting before then.

So what did she expect? Gemma asked herself depressedly. He had made the position perfectly clear on his departure. Why couldn't she simply accept it and get on with the rest of her life?

Because she loved him, came the answer, and love couldn't be brushed aside as easily as that. Deep down she would go on hoping for a long time to come.

They were all booked on the same afternoon flight to Heathrow. On impulse, Gemma asked the young woman holding the seat number next to her mother to change places with her, drawing a surprised but not averse glance from the latter.

'Won't Jason be lonely without you?' she asked. 'The two of you have been inseparable since Logan left.'

Gemma smiled and shook her head. 'It isn't that kind of relationship. Anyway, he has the girl I just turned out of here to entertain.' She fastened her seat-belt, settling herself comfortably as the plane began taxiing out to the runway. 'Where are you going to be living?' she asked.

'I have my old suite at the Savoy,' Adele acknowledged, her head back against the rest. 'I made sure of that before I left New York.'

'Supposing *Kate* turns into a long run?'

'How do you mean, suppose? I've never been in anything else but!'

There was always a first time, thought Gemma. Logan was gambling on a lavish production with special stage effects and magnificent costumes to draw the crowds, which was why the costs were running so high. Just to break even at the box office was going to take capacity houses those vital first weeks.

'What I really meant was shall you be staying on at the Savoy?' she said, changing tack. 'I'd have thought a service apartment might——'

'I prefer hotels. I always have.' It was Adele's turn to change the subject. 'Who is this Sally Rogers?'

'A friend of Logan's,' Gemma touched the collar of the pink suit. 'She owns the boutique where I bought this, and most of my other clothes—at least, where Logan bought them.'

'I wondered about that. If you had to do this thing you did why couldn't you use the money I sent you? Surely that had to be better than letting a man you didn't even know keep you!' Adele paused, head still in the same position on the backrest. 'You *were* living with him, weren't you?'

'Not for long.' Gemma fought to keep depression at bay. 'I'll pay him back every penny he ever spent on me as soon as I can.'

'You could do it now except that you'd apparently rather owe Logan than be under any obligation to your own mother.'

'That isn't true.'

'Then prove it. You must have some idea of what everything cost. If you haven't I'm sure this Sally person could tell you. Write him a cheque and have done with it.' The red head moved when Gemma failed to answer, her eyes concealed behind the dark glasses. 'You see, I was right!'

'All right!' The words were dragged from her. 'I'll do it. He isn't going to like it, but I'll do it anyway.'

'Good. The sooner the better. You were through anyway. This will make it a clean break.'

She had a good point, Gemma conceded as the plane began its turn on to the runway. She would feel better about things when the financial side was cleared up. She was going to have to delve into her bank balance in any case to pay Sally rent until she was earning.

'You know,' she said suddenly, 'you haven't called me *darling* once while we've been talking.'

'Of course not.' The answering smile was faint. 'I never waste a performance. Hold my hand, will you? I hate take-offs.'

There was a whole lot they each needed to learn about the other, reflected Gemma, complying with the request. They might never be close as parent and child should be, but they could perhaps achieve some measure of understanding.

The whole party split up at the airport. Jason was going back to Sevenoaks with his father and Caryn for a couple of nights.

'I've a feeling I'm going to be the pig in the middle,' Jason confided, saying a temporary goodbye to Gemma. 'Caryn isn't happy. He'd be better off without her, if only he could see it!'

'He'll work it out,' she said.

'In other words, leave him to do it. Too right!' He laughed and bent to kiss her swiftly and lightly on the lips. 'See you Friday at the theatre.'

Sally was expecting her. She left the shop in charge of the two assistants and took Gemma upstairs to the small but comfortable flat.

'I could have let it a hundred times over since it came empty,' she said after showing her the bedroom and kitchenette, 'only I'm choosy about who I have living over the premises. Any idea how long you'll be needing it?'

'Not yet,' Gemma admitted. 'If you'll tell me the rent I'll pay you the first month.'

Sally shrugged. 'Logan has already taken care of it.' She watched Gemma bite her lip, added casually, 'I suppose he thought he owed you that much consideration after leaving you out there the way he did. I'm not sure what it was all about and I don't particularly want to know. If you'll take a word of advice, you'll leave things the way they are.'

'I can't,' said Gemma. 'Not where money is concerned. Do you think you could tell me just how much he spent on my clothes?'

'Nothing yet. I only got round to totting up the final bill a couple of days ago, and I haven't seen him since. I'll probably send it to him if he doesn't contact me this week.'

'I can save you the trouble. Give me the figure and I'll get round to the bank first thing in the morning. I—er—need a new cheque book.'

The other's brows lifted. 'Are you sure about this? You might have a shock.'

'Quite sure,' said Gemma firmly.

'Okay then. Make yourself at home while I go fetch my book. There's coffee in the kitchen if you feel like some.'

Gemma did. She had the kettle boiling before Sally returned. Taking the tray through to the little sitting room, she set it down on the coffee table and sat down herself, holding out her hand for the paper Sally held. 'Please.'

It was a lengthy bill, neatly itemised. The lower figure took Gemma's breath away for a moment. Sally watched her with a certain amusement.

'I did warn you. None of my stuff comes cheap. Logan can well afford it, and he was the one who wanted you kitted out.'

'I can pay it.' Gemma folded the bill and put it in her purse, reaching for her coffee. 'Would you consider sending Logan a cheque for the rent he paid you and let me settle that too?'

'Sorry.' The refusal was firm. 'You're going to have to sort that one out yourself. I'm going to be in enough trouble as it is for giving you that!'

It was time to change the subject. 'Why don't you live in the flat yourself?' asked Gemma. 'I'd have thought it would be ideal from a business point of view.'

Sally shrugged. 'I spend a lot of time on buying trips so it would be empty anyway. I share a house with a friend who can look after things when I'm not there. Apart from that, I like to keep business and personal life strictly separate.' She drained her coffee cup and stood up. 'I'd better get back. I'm in the middle of pricing a new consignment of wool and mohair separates from Germany for my autumn and winter range. You should take a look. They're very exclusive.'

Expensive too, no doubt, thought Gemma dryly as her landlady left. Anyone who could charge forty-five pounds for a simple pair of cotton trousers had to be on the make. Or was it simply she who was out of touch with prices?

Unpacking in the bedroom, she found herself regarding every item of clothing with new eyes. They were well made, she had to grant that. They darned well had to be, because they were going to have to last her a long time. For certain, her winter wardrobe was going to be nowhere near as extensive!

The shop closed for the day at five-thirty. Sally phoned through on the extension before she left.

'I stocked up the fridge if you feel like cooking yourself a meal,' she said. 'You should have everything you need for a couple of days.'

'Your idea or Logan's?' asked Gemma, and heard the faint sigh.

'Mine, if you must know. I'll add it on to next quarter's rent! See you.'

Gemma put down the receiver with unnecessary force. A quarter? He had paid a whole quarter in advance! Lord only knew what that would come to! At this rate she was going to be close to cleaning out an account she had sworn never to touch again. No matter how long a run the show had, Bianca was never going to see her clear of debt.

She cooked a steak and made a salad for supper, taking a tray through to the sitting room to switch on the television for the six o'clock news. The comparison with activities over the past fortnight was ludicrous. At this time yesterday they had all been sitting on deck with cool drinks to hand and the warm breeze caressing bare arms. They'd had more dull grey skies and rain here in England over the past couple of weeks, by all accounts.

It was being so alone she found hard to take. Logan's comings and goings at the studio had been unpredictable, but there had always been some part of the twenty-four hours when he was with her. She would settle happily for that same arrangement right now.

Washing up for one took little time at all. Afterwards she found pencil and paper and sat down on the sofa to make out a list of requirements for the morning. First the bank, to sort out her exact financial position. From what she recalled of her last statement, she had around two thousand pounds to her credit. It still went against the grain to touch it, but what was the alternative? She could pay all her debts and start clear. One thing she must make sure of, though: there must be no further contributions from her mother.

She had left the television on for company. At first she thought the sound of a doorbell ringing was coming from the set. Only when it was insistently repeated did the truth penetrate. There were two entrances to the flat: one through the shop, to which Sally held the only key, the other at the rear through the kitchen. There was a bolt and chain on the solid-looking door, instilling a certain caution where none had previously existed.

'Who is it?' she called.

'Logan,' came the answer.

She opened up with fingers gone suddenly nerveless, her heart lifting to the very sight of him standing there on the step. He was wearing the dark grey shadow-stripe she remembered so well, his shirt whiter than white against the tan of his face. She wanted him with an insistency and intensity that knotted her insides.

'You'd better come in,' she said, surprised that she could sound so normal. 'I wasn't expecting anyone.'

'Me least of all?' he suggested, responding to the invitation. Grey eyes looked her over, expression veiled. 'I had a phone call from Sally.'

Gemma looked back at him steadily. 'And?'

'And we have matters to discuss. Supposing we do it in comfort.'

'Of course.' She turned to lead the way, pausing in the doorway. 'Would you like some coffee? I can't offer you anything stronger. I don't have anything in.'

'I don't need a drink,' he said, 'of any kind.'

The sitting room was dim. Gemma switched on a lamp and turned off the television before sitting down on the sofa. Logan had taken the chair a couple of feet away. He wasted no time beating about the bush.

'We had a deal, if you remember. Leaving aside this bill of Sally's for the moment, I still owe you two hundred pounds.'

'Which I've told you more than once I don't want,' Gemma responded. 'I never really did. Initially I was only interested in wheedling my way into an audition.'

'Until you got side-tracked. Yes, I know.'

'But you still don't entirely believe it?'

He shrugged. 'I believe we had enough going for us to split your interests. Don't try confusing the issue, Gemma. I'm here because Sally told me you were insisting on paying for the clothes you wouldn't have bought if it hadn't been for me.'

'She had no right!'

'She had every right. She knows I can afford her prices.'

'So can I.'

'I said afford, not just pay. Anyway, that's not the point. It's my debt. If you want to give the whole damned lot to Oxfam you can go right ahead and do it, but I'll take that bill Sally gave you.'

'It isn't just me,' said Gemma after a lengthy moment of indecision. 'I half promised my mother I'd straighten things out.'

'Supplying the wherewithal doesn't give her any entitlement to insist.' Logan made a sudden impatient movement. 'For God's sake, let's finish it! I'm sick of the whole subject!'

He wasn't alone in that. She already wished she had never begun it. The billhead was tucked between the pages of the notebook in which she had been jotting her list. She took it out and handed it to him, tensing to the very touch of his fingertips.

'If that's all you came for, you have it,' she said thickly. 'Thanks for the telegram, by the way. You went to a lot of trouble.'

He didn't answer straight away, studying her face with an expression she wouldn't allow herself to define in case she was wrong. Time elapsed had made little difference to the effect he had on her senses. Even just sitting there looking at her he set her on fire.

'I told myself that's all I was coming for,' he said at last, on a note of resignation. 'I should have known better. Right this minute I can't think of a single thing more important than making love to you.'

'Then why don't you?' she whispered.

He shed his jacket before coming over to her, loosening his tie and slinging it over the back of the sofa as he sat down beside her. She went into his arms like a bird coming home to roost, mouth lifting, clinging; desperately seeking. He had taken advantage of the first excuse to see her; that had to mean somethng.

He undressed her slowly, pausing to kiss and caress each portion of flesh he exposed; devouring her with lips and tongue and teeth until she moaned for relief. She was scarcely aware of his own gradual shedding of clothing, only of the ultimate feel of his body on hers, of the vital bonding she wanted never to end.

'I've thought about this every night since I left the yacht,' Logan murmured later when they lay limp and spent in each other's arms. 'I never had too many principles to start with, but you've undermined them all! Just don't let me down on Friday.'

'I won't,' she promised. 'I'll dance the way I never danced before!'

'You'd better. I'm going out on a limb for you in more ways than one.' He stirred, lifting a wrist to glance at his watch. 'I have to get moving.'

Gemma felt the pain run through her like a knife. 'Already?'

'I'm afraid so. I have an appointment at half past eight.' His lips nuzzled her temple, pushing aside the heavy fringe of hair. 'I'm tied up tomorrow too, but I could make it around seven again.'

'Another hour to fill in?' Her voice shook. 'I'd as soon pay my dues in cash!'

There was a moment of rigidity before he shoved himself upright to reach for his clothes. Gemma lay motionless as he got to his feet and made for the bathroom. Only when the door was forcefully closed did she move to sit up.

Her housecoat was in the bedroom. She gathered her things from the floor and took them with her, tossing them on to the bed. The cotton clung to her damp skin. As soon as Logan had gone she would take a long hot shower and wash the very memory away. He wasn't coming back— that much she was certain about. She had made herself too available—too easy. Only never again. From now on he satisfied his appetites elsewhere.

He was drawing on his jacket when she went back to the sitting room. The glance he gave her was totally unemotional.

'Just one more thing,' she said coolly. 'I pay my own rent. That way I'm at least entitled to keep my door shut!'

'Anything you like.' He sounded indifferent. 'Send me a cheque.'

'I don't know the amount.'

'Sally will tell you if you ask her.'

'I'm sure Sally could tell me a whole lot if I asked her. How long did you allocate *her* in her day?'

'Drop it,' he advised. 'I'll see you at the theatre Friday. Ten o'clock sharp. Your mother asked to be there by the way. That should put you on your mettle.'

He was going. Suddenly and perversely Gemma wanted him to stay. An hour, two hours—what did it matter? She would have had something, now she had nothing.

Pride kept her silent. It was too late to change her mind. She locked and bolted the door after him and slid the chain, standing with her face pressed against the wood while she fought back the tears. He wasn't worth it. He simply wasn't worth it! She had to convince herself of that.

Friday was sunny and warm, mocking the forecasts the way only British weather could. The stage doorman ticked off Gemma's name on a list before waving her on through to the dingy backstage corridors. She could use number three dressing room, he told her.

Gemma was wearing a leotard under her skirt and blouse. She slipped the latter garments off swiftly and donned the flexible slippers, then did a few limbering-up exercises to calm her nerves. It needed another ten minutes to the hour, but there was no way she could wait around in here.

From the wings she would be able to see just who was out there waiting to judge her.

Jason was there before her. He looked as tense as she felt.

'Your mother's here, did you know?' he said. 'That makes four of them down there.'

So Logan had come. But then he had to, hadn't he? The two of them were here at all only because he had brought pressure to bear on his associates.

The front stalls house lights were up. By moving forward a little Gemma could see the split group seated in the middle section, two to the sixth and two to the seventh rows. Logan sat behind with Adele, leaving director and choreographer to their own discourse. He was smiling at something Adele was saying, no shade of strain about the lean features. Gemma felt resolve harden inside her. She would show him. They would both show him! He was doing them no favours.

'It's bang on ten,' said Jason. 'Let's show our faces.'

Jean Scott got to her feet as they walked onstage, beckoning them down to the footlights. She was a tall, spare woman with a plain face devoid of make-up and hair scragged back into a rough knot at her nape, but she still moved with the dancer's lightness of tread.

'We're going to need to see you both solo and together,' she said. 'Tell Jerry over there at the piano what you want.' She nodded briskly. 'Let's get started.'

It was a long and exhausting twenty minutes, with little time to consider anything beyond the immediate demands. Gemma believed they had both of them put up a creditable solo performance, but it wasn't until halfway through their shared number that she really began to feel they were getting there. Dancing with Jason was like dancing with her own shadow; they were attuned; sensitive to every minute variation of body angle and step. They were both running with perspiration when they finished, but they knew they had acquitted themselves well.

The silence after the pianist stopped playing seemed to drum in Gemma's ears. The four down in the stalls weren't even looking at them, talking among themselves in low tones. Jean Scott was the first to move, coming up on stage.

'I want you both to try something for me,' she said. 'I'll show you the sequence, you copy. No music.'

Gemma followed the complicated pattern of movement with concentration, glanced at Jason for confirmation, then launched herself along the same path knowing he was right at her back.

'And again,' ordered the choreographer without a flicker of reaction.

Three times in all they obeyed that instruction. The final time their tutor herself joined in, grinning when the three of them finished in perfect line.

'Okay,' she said, looking out across the footlights to where the others sat watching. 'I guess that's it so far as I'm concerned. Everybody in agreement?' The latter question was apparently rhetorical—at least she didn't bother waiting for an answer, turning back to the two on stage. 'Rehearsals start the week after next. We've got seven weeks to opening, and we're going to need all of them.' She paused, glancing from face to face with quizzical expression. 'Nothing to say?'

'We're lost for words,' Jason acknowledged. He slid an arm about Gemma's shoulders and hugged her, the laughter sparkling in his eyes. 'But not for long! We'll give it all we've got, eh, Gem?'

'All!' she echoed. Her eyes were on the three still in the stalls. Logan wasn't even going to acknowledge her. Yet why should she care? She had what she really wanted.

Changing back into street clothes proved something of an anti-climax. Gemma was fastening the last button when her mother walked into the cramped dressing room.

'So Robert gets his way,' she said. 'It's going to be a family affair. Congratulations. You're an excellent dancer.'

Meeting the green eyes so like her own, Gemma knew a swift pang of sympathy. To be forced to acknowledge a twenty-two-year-old daughter was bad enough; to have that same daughter right alongside on stage must be infinitely worse.

'There'll never be another Adele Berrisford,' she said. 'We're following different paths.'

'But you're going to be singing too. How about the Tom, Dick or Harry number?'

Gemma laughed. 'It hardly needs a great voice—I imagine that's why they didn't bother asking me to try it out. I don't sing as such. I'm not even interested in singing. I can carry a tune and I can project—that just about says it all.' Her tone softened. 'Nobody else can touch you, much less me!'

Her mother's smile came faintly. 'Thanks. You see, it's all I really care about, being on top. There's no one man can ever give me anything to compare.'

It was a moment before Gemma answered. When she did it was obliquely. 'Is Logan taking you to lunch?'

'As a matter of fact, no. I have another engagement. So did he.' Still she hesitated. 'I asked him if you'd settled with him yet, but I never got an answer. Don't you think——'

'It's being sorted out.' Gemma could think of no other way of evading the issue. Obeying an instinct, she went and put her lips lightly to her mother's cheek. 'Thanks for coming round to see me. What would you prefer I called you, by the way? Mother sounds too formal, and you're hardly the "Mom" type.' The last with a smile. 'I suppose there's always "Miss Berrisford".'

'You'd better just make it Adele.' For a brief moment there was an odd faraway look in her eyes. 'You know, at times, you're so like your father.' She briskened again immediately. 'I have to go. Take care of yourself. If you need me you know where to reach me.'

Gemma let her go. This was not the time to mention money. If the monthly credit came through as usual then she would take the appropriate steps. In the meantime she would be looking round for somewhere else to live. At six hundred pounds a quarter the flat was probably reasonable by central London standards, but it wasn't where she wanted to be. She had mailed Logan the cheque, and would take the loss should something suitable turn up before the three months expired.

The very thought of Logan brought bitterness in its wake. So don't think of him, she told herself. From now on she took a leaf out of her mother's book and concentrated on her career.

Jason was waiting for her by the stage door. 'Your mother has just left,' he said. 'She seemed to have things on her mind. No trouble between the two of you?'

'Nothing we can't get over in time,' Gemma acknowledged. She smiled into the brown eyes. 'How does it feel to be in work again?'

'The same way it feels for you, I imagine. Absolutely fantastic!' He took her arm as he opened the door, urging her through ahead. 'What plans do you have for today?'

'None.' She was looking towards the street, only vaguely aware of the engine starting up at the back of the alleyway. 'What did you have in mind?'

The Mercedes reached them before Jason could answer. Logan had the nearside window already down.

'I want to talk to you,' he said.

'Both of us?' asked Jason, and received a grim smile.

'Just do me a favour and take off, will you. Gemma, get in.'

Had she been wavering to start with the tone would have resolved her. 'No, thanks,' she said stiffly. 'I'd rather walk.'

He didn't argue, just got out of the car and came round the front, blocking escape.

'I hope you're not going to try any heroics,' he advised Jason on an ironic note. 'You'll only be delaying the inevitable, because I'm taking her with me whether you like it or not!'

'Whether I like it or not isn't the point, is it?' responded the younger man. 'The choice is Gemma's.'

Eyes on her face, Logan reached out a hand and opened the passenger door. For a moment Gemma resisted, then was lost. She gave a tiny sigh and slid into the seat, looking up at Jason with apology and a silent plea for understanding.

'I'll see you next week.'

He shrugged and walked off, not looking back. Logan got back behind the wheel and set the car in motion, turning left at the alley entrance into the mid-morning traffic.

'Square one,' he said. 'Let's see if we can make a better job of it this time.'

Gemma was silent, neither daring or caring to jump to any conclusions. She spoke only when they crossed the river.

'We're going to the studio?'

'It's where we're going to be living,' he said. 'Better get used to it.'

Warmth was spreading cautiously through her. 'You take a lot for granted.'

'I know.' He sounded suddenly rueful. 'Too much. I've spent the last thirty-six hours figuring myself out.'

'With what conclusion?'

'That I'm capable of loving one woman to the exclusion of all others.' The glance he gave her was swift yet all-encompassing. 'But only if it's you. Does that have any similarity to the way you feel about me?'

'More than a little.' She put out a hand and rested it for a fleeting moment on his thigh, feeling the muscle tense beneath her fingers, her senses stir in unison. 'I love you so much it hurts!'

His mouth slanted. 'I know *that* feeling too. Incidentally, if you plan on doing that again give me fair warning. You almost had us in the river!'

Gemma laughed, following the movement of his lips with her eyes, remembering the feel of them on hers. 'I can wait. Just!' The laughter died, uncertainty suddenly returning. 'Logan, it's so quick. Are you sure it's love you're talking about?'

He drew the car to a halt at the rear of the line waiting for the lights to change before answering. 'Want me to prove it?'

'Can you?' she asked softly.

'The best way I know,' he said, 'is with tangible evidence. Open the glove compartment.'

They were moving again before she could bring herself to do so, her heart thudding to the recollection of another time not so long ago. The same small cream box lay there. Or was it? She reached out a hand gone clumsy to pick it up and fumble it open, gazing at the sapphire and diamond hoop in a heady mixture of relief and elation.

'It isn't the same,' was all she could find to say in that first delirious moment.

'I should hope not.' Logan was watching the traffic ahead, a smile curving his lips. 'I might not be capable of doing the whole knee-bending bit, but I'm not crass enough to give you a ring we used as a prop.' The pause was brief. 'Am I taking too much for granted again?'

'No. Oh no!' Her eyes were turned to him, bright shining green, her mouth soft and tremulous. 'I thought you said you weren't the marrying kind?'

'I didn't think I was until I met you. Even then, it took me a while to adjust my ideas.'

'So what decided you in the end?'

'You did,' he said. 'The other night. You made me take a really good look at myself—and where I was going. I'd always thought of marriage as putting one's head in a noose, only I can see now that it depends on the fit. Apart from the physical side of things, I can live with you, Gemma. You don't bore me into the ground with trivialities; you don't fill the place with feminine clutter.'

Give me time! she thought humorously, hiding her smile. He was still the chauvinist—still so sure of his masculine lack of pedestrianism in any sphere! But she loved him anyway.

'I don't know what my mother's going to say,' she remarked.

'It isn't your mother I'm marrying,' he pointed out with indisputable logic. His smile came and went. 'She's going to make a rare in-law!'

And a rarer grandmother, thought Gemma fleetingly. Logan would change his mind on that score too in time to come. She knew it with a certainty she could not have explained. She longed to reach the studio, to be in his arms again. A whole new world was opening up before her.

It was summer again, a dryer, warmer summer than the year before. The river sparkled in the morning sunlight, flowing swift and smooth towards the heights of Tower Bridge visible in the distance.

Gemma cut a spray from the tumbling waterfall of pink clematis covering one wall, and placed it in the shallow bowl of water at the centre of the breakfast table. Being able to eat outside was a bonus most central London dwellers lacked. If the studio had its drawbacks, she should consider herself fortunate in that respect at least.

Logan came out carrying the Sunday newspapers. He had shaved, but was still wearing the silk robe and leather slippers he preferred when relaxing at home.

'Late to bed and late to rise!' he said with some satisfaction, taking a seat. 'It might not catch any early worms, but it's the finest way out of spending a weekend.' His glance slid over her, the smile reminiscent. 'Especially considering the extras!'

'Not extra,' Gemma corrected lightly. 'Part of. I'll fetch your victuals, oh, master!'

He caught her round the waist as she moved past him, pulling her down on to his knees and nuzzling her neck. 'Know thy place, wench.'

'My place is with thee, my lord, my life, my keeper!' She was laughing, fingers tangling in the dark hair as she put her lips to his forehead. 'Don't you want to eat?'

'Only you,' he said, brushing aside the material of her *peignoir* to follow the line of her collarbone. 'The bacon can wait.'

She could have pointed out that at this moment they were in full view of passing river traffic, but she knew that wouldn't stop him. To hell with it anyway. As he said, the bacon could wait.

The blow-up mattress she used for sunbathing

made a more than adequate bed. Down below the level of the balustrade they were in a private world of their own, with only the birds to see them. There was the ease of familiarity in their lovemaking, yet no diminution of passion. Wherever and whenever, it was always good.

They lay for a long time afterwards, replete in the sun. Gemma made the first reluctant move.

'Just because we don't have a matinee to worry about it doesn't mean we can spend the whole day lazing around,' she reminded him. 'You said you had things to do this afternoon.'

'Things *we* have to do.' He made no attempt to let her go, lying with an arm and a leg comfortably extended across her, eyes closed. 'It's a nice day for looking at houses.'

It was a moment or two before she could gather herself to speak. 'Houses?' she managed at last, hardly daring to hope he might mean what he appeared to mean. 'For us?'

'Who else?' His tone was lazy, his eyes still closed. 'This place was fine in my bachelor days, but it's beginning to feel too temporary. We'll keep it on, of course. It's handy to have somewhere to stay in town. I thought west of London for preference. On the river, if possible. We've two appointments to view after lunch.'

Gemma lifted herself on an elbow, shrugging off the weight of his arm without even noticing. 'Do you mean to tell me you've planned it all without saying a solitary word!'

'Now wouldn't that have spoiled the surprise?' He opened one eye to squint at her face, the smile slowly spreading. 'You're irresistible when you're angry—do you know that?'

Gemma tried to still the laughter bubbling up inside her, but it was hopeless—the way he was hopeless. She would never change him. But then would she want to change him? Would he be the man she loved if he were any different?

'How long have you been thinking about buying a house?' she asked, casting resentment aside. 'What kind of places are they, these two? When——'

'Hold it!' He was laughing himself, shaking his head. 'One at a time!' He paused to look at her, putting up an unexpected hand to smooth the side of her face with a touch so tender it brought a lump to her throat. 'I got to wondering about the future,' he said softly. 'The show looks set for the rest of the year, and the new production's well in hand, but there's more to life than work. How would you feel about taking a Sabbatical when *Kate* comes off, and going in for another kind of production?'

She had been right, Gemma thought, feeling the glow start deep. She had known all along that this day would come. 'I'd like it,' she said in a tone as soft as his own. 'I'd really like it!'

'I thought you might.' Just for a moment there was a certain hesitation in the grey eyes. 'Gemma, you're not likely to turn into one of those women who devote their whole lives to their children, are you?'

'As if you'd let me,' she said with a smile, 'even if I wanted to!'

'That's true.' He pulled her down to him and kissed her, holding her close with a sigh of content. 'And to think I almost passed you by that day on the road! Just another silly kid asking for trouble, I told myself.'

'And look what I finished up with!' There was a lengthy pause before she said on a different note, 'You know, you never did tell me what you were doing at the theatre with Caryn that night.'

'So I didn't.' He sounded amused. 'And it's taken you nearly ten months to get round to asking. That's what I call forbearance!'

'It's what I call politic. I've been waiting for the right moment.'

'You consider this is it?'

'No,' she acknowledged. 'I just can't wait any longer.' She lifted her head again to look into his eyes, seeing the smile deepen. 'So?'

'There's not much to it,' he said. 'She phoned to say she was in town for the evening and wanted to see me. I did some hasty phoning of my own and managed to get a couple of cancellations. I put her into a taxi and sent her home about four minutes after we left the theatre. Much, I might add, against her will.'

'I'm glad yours was strong enough.'

'It didn't need to be. Not in the sense you're talking about. We were finished before she ever met Robert.'

Gemma pulled a wry face. 'I feel so sorry for Robert. He really did love her.'

'But he's better off without her in the long run. I think he'd be the first to admit it now.' His tone altered, taking on a gruffer note. 'Just as I'd be the first to admit that I couldn't take it if you ever left me. Keep telling me you love me, Gemma. I need the reassurance.'

She told him, though not in words. Words never said enough.

Harlequin® Plus

A WORD ABOUT THE AUTHOR

Kay Thorpe has always been able to spin a yarn. In fact according to her teachers, she says, she was the best storyteller in the whole school, particularly when it came to finding excuses for being late! But in her teens she didn't see herself as a potential author. Writing was just a hobby then, an outlet for her imagination. She found that on paper she could go anywhere and be anything she wanted.

When she left school in 1952 she couldn't make up her mind about the kind of job she wanted to do, so she tried "just about everything," including training as a dental nurse and joining the Women's Royal Air Force to become an oral hygenist. Marriage, domesticity and motherhood took care of another few years before she began to feel the need for an additional interest in her life. It was then that she first began to think seriously about writing as a career.

She hit the jackpot with her first completed novel—a fact she marvels at still, especially since she had to laboriously type the manuscript with two fingers! Nonetheless, the book was accepted, and she became a romance novelist. As she puts it, "I had found my niche at last!"